One Hundred Birds

Telling One Hundred Little Stories

*

Kristina Henson

Cover design and illustrations by Kristina Henson.

ISBN: 978-0-578-21869-4

Like most things I do, this is dedicated to you, Lily.

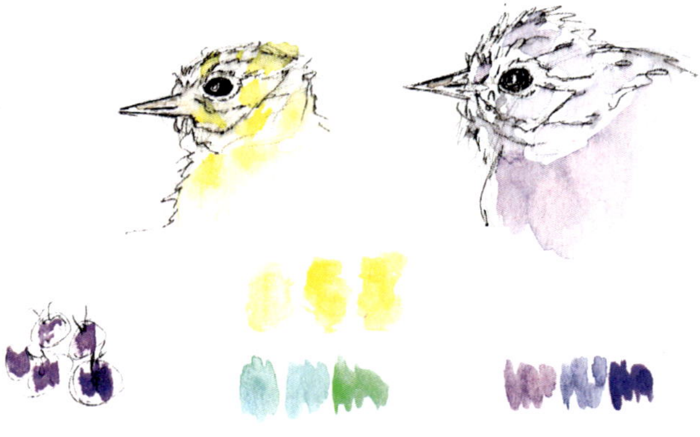

The Berry Man

A net is thrown over the berries that he sells
from his front yard.
He sits in a nylon lawn chair behind a card table
with the containers of berries in a neat row.
I could have eaten them if it wasn't for the net.
It feels cruel to booby trap the highlight of my
summer snacking.

He takes a break and walks one block to the statue
of Mary behind the Saint Francis rectory.
He bows his head, places a hand on the cold statue.
His rosary beads hang down and sway around Mary's hands.
Lips move.
He prays.
I watch from the roof.
I watch from the tree branch.
I follow him home.
The berries, still covered, are out of my reach.
I shit on his car.

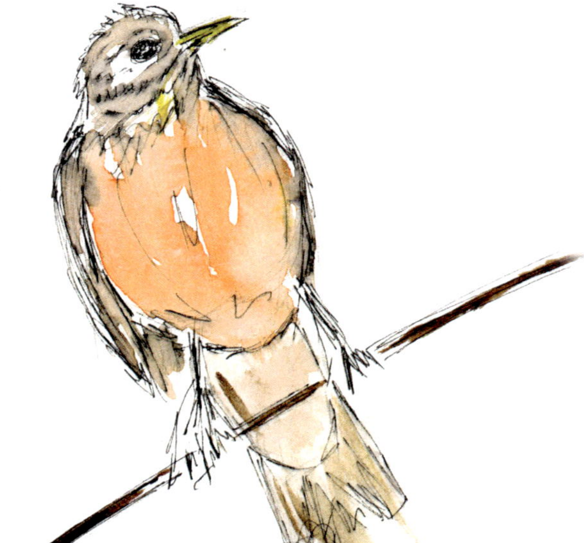

Big Mama

This morning, when I was at the bird feeder and the suction
cups fell off the window and everything fell to the ground,
you called me a fatso mama bird. That hurt. You think it's
easy or slimming to have a belly full of robin eggs?
I don't mock you when you limp around the yard in your
sweatpants. Or do I?

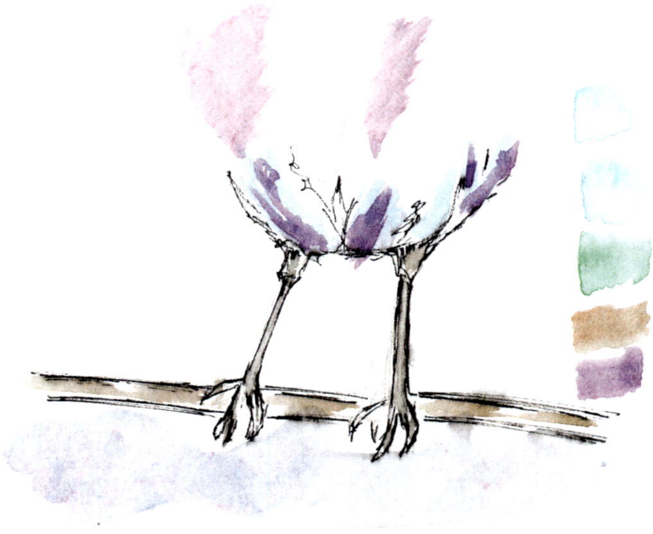

Little Feet

Five things these twiggy
little feet have never done:

Worn socks.
Had a pedicure.
Played kickball.
Danced the Hokey Pokey.
The morning after walk of shame.

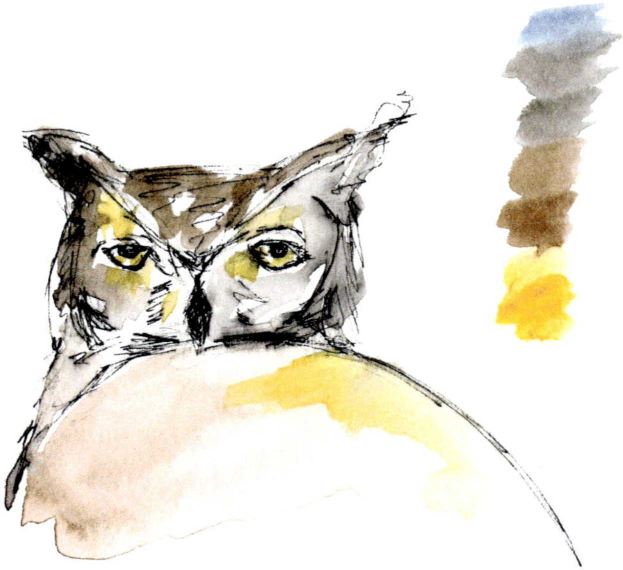

Hoot

It's a game we play
Just you and I
In the dark
I hoot
You look
I hide
I hoot
You look
I hide
You give up and go inside
I kill a mouse and leave it on your doorstep
You blame the cat
I win

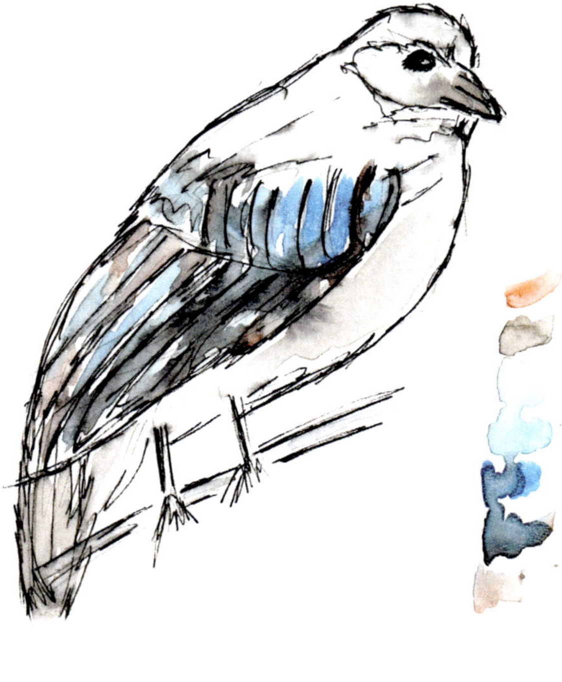

Wings

Give your children wings to fly. Why do you say that?
They aren't birds. Give them feet to walk out the door
and a gas card. Leave the flying bit to us.

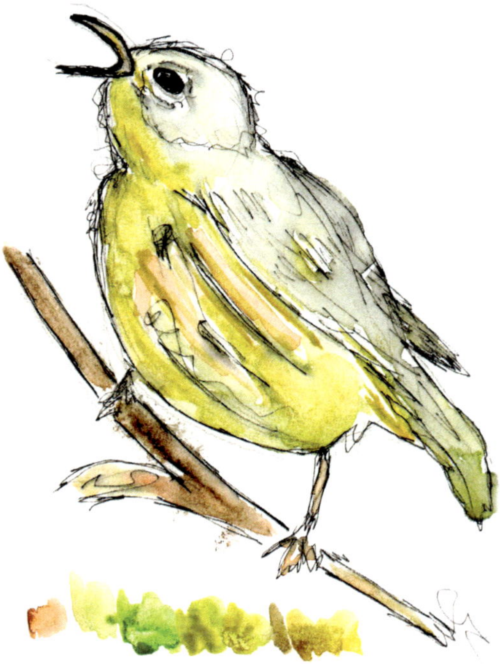

Early Riser

Banging on the bedroom window?
A little dramatic, don't you think?

A few weeks ago, when I was building
a nest next to your bedroom window,
you thought it was adorable.
I can't control it.
I wake up with so much gratitude.
I need to sing.
Praise to you almighty God.
Thank you thank you thank you,
for the air I breathe and this healthy body,
for my friends and family,
for these gorgeous wings and gift of flight.
Tweet
Tweet
Tweet
Tweet
Tweet

You lay in bed with a pillow over your head.
Whispering.
Burn in Hell songbird.
It's still dark.
Go back to sleep.

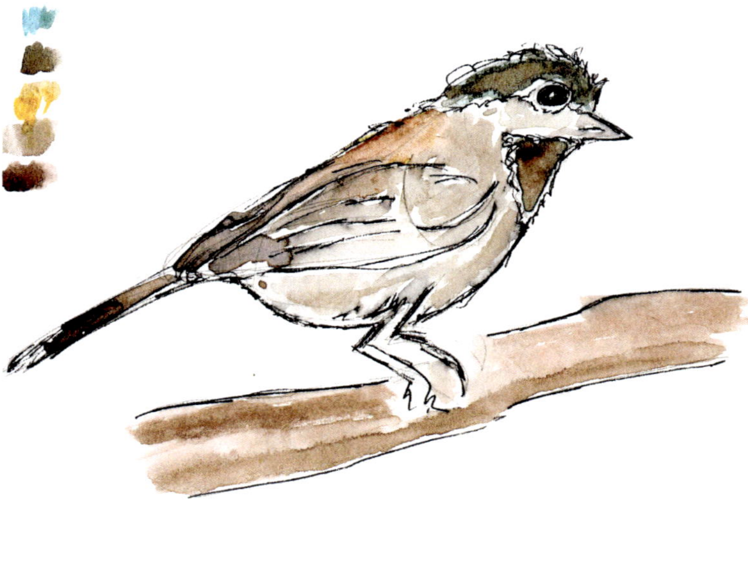

For Nana

Every time you see me your thoughts
drift to years past.
Big holidays.
Walks in the woods.
Hot pink.
Cold celery and carrot sticks.
Scrap paper and crayons in the hall closet.
The way she sometimes smelled like white wine
and crisp apples.
"Oh, look at those darling little Chickadees
at the feeder" she would say.
"Look at those darling Chickadees at the feeder" you say.
No one hears you but me. And maybe Nana.

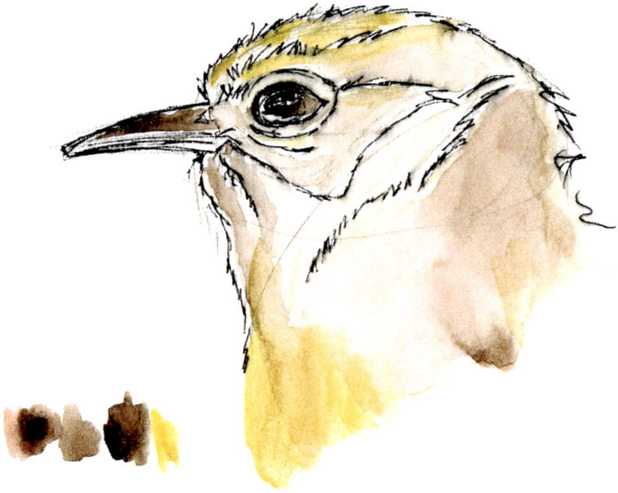

Spring Cleaning

Thud
Oh crud
I'm covered in mud

What the heck was that?
I'm being laughed at by the cat

Who watches from the window ledge
As I stumble away from the overgrown hedge

I can't believe I fell
I think you cleaned those windows a little too well

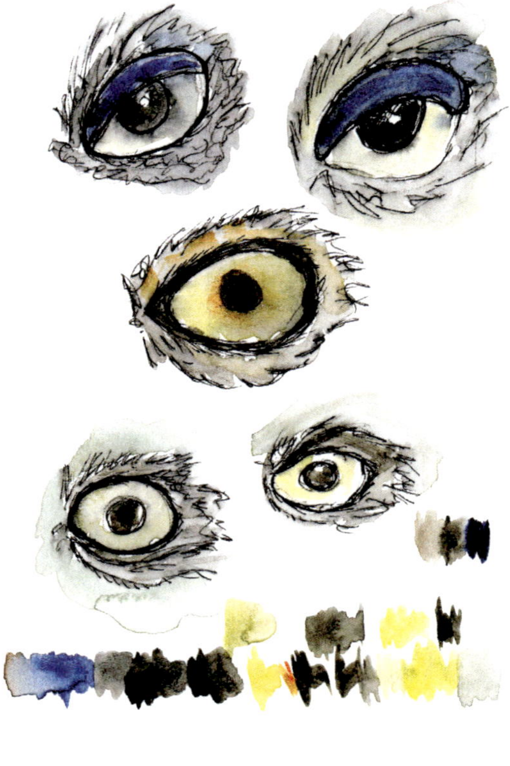

Eye Spy

I spy
With my own little bird eye
Someone washing the dishes
Who desperately wishes
Time would slow down for a tad
You look stark raving mad
Feeling so sad
Virginia is just down the road
Count your blessings that time hasn't slowed

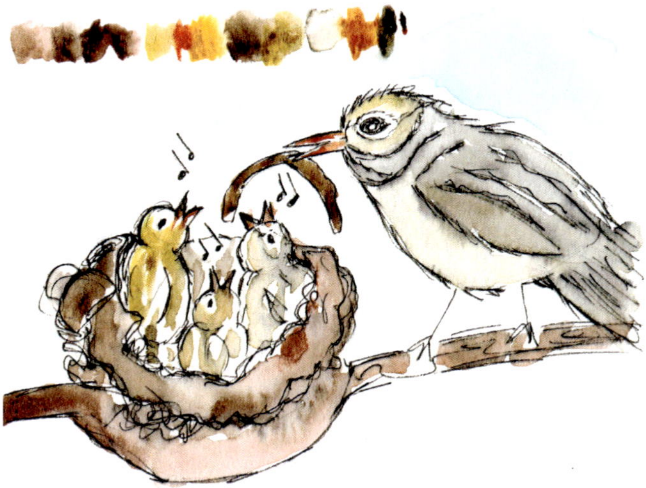

Welcome Home

After work, getting inside the house doesn't seem so easy for you. They're all right there at the back door. 2 cats, 1 dog. 1 kid. The cats pace. Meow meow meow. It seems like they conspired on this all day. "You run between her legs, to the right, I'll lay in front of her, the dogs jumps, she trips, bam, she's down. Take the can of cat food and run." Why are they trying to kill you? None of those fools can open that can without you.

The dog jumps up to give you a hug. He needs to pee. Bad. Go quickly before he pees on your feet .

That beautiful, sweetish kid wants to talk about her day and you want to hear her. Take a deep breath. Take the dog out. Hug the kid. Put your slippers on. Feed the cats. Hug the kid again. Throwing a worm in my nest? It is so easy.

Welcome home.

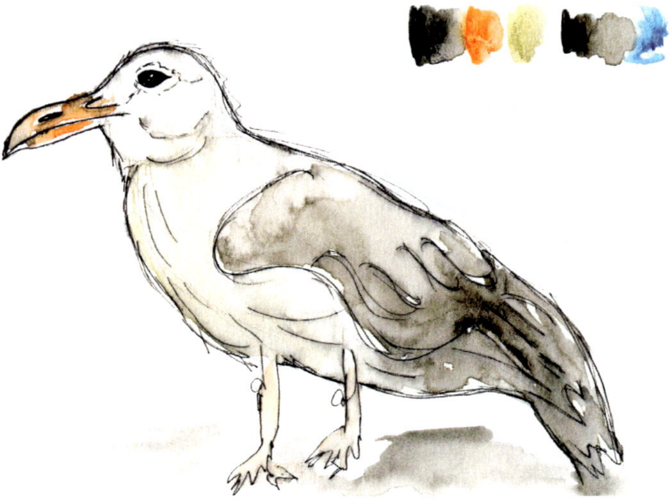

The Walmart Seagull

No, I'm not confused. I didn't land here in the Walmart
parking lot thinking it was a lake. Give me a little credit.
I'm no crow but I'm not a complete moron either.
Annoying, yes. Mistaking asphalt for water, umm, no. At
the beach, I have to perform this Olympic level swoop down,
scare the pants off a kid, and snatch technique for ONE
cheese doodle. Here, toddlers leave this store throwing fits
and food like you have never seen. It's an all-day buffet of
goldfish crackers and anything else their parents tried
to bribe them with for silence. I snack and snack and snack.
Then I work on my poobomb dropping skills.
Duck and dodge shoppers.
Duck and dodge.
This is the American Dream.

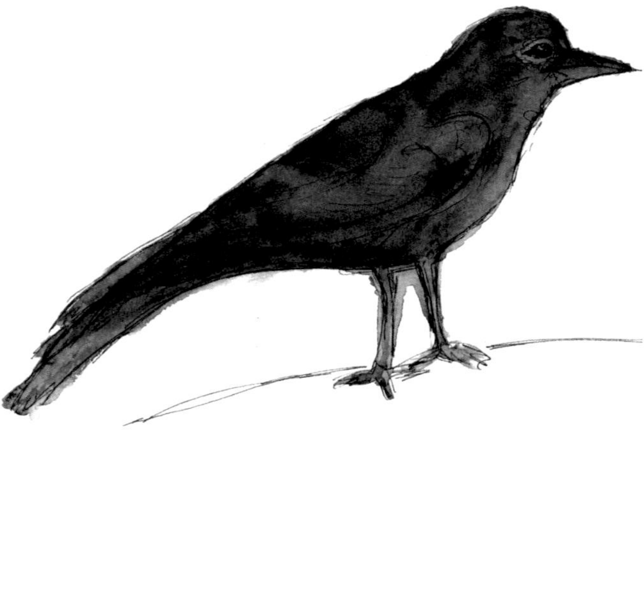

Smart Guy

It's me. The Crow. The smart one the Seagull from Walmart was talking about yesterday.

You know that feeling you get every garbage day when I'm sitting defiantly on the lid of your can? That feeling that I'm watching your every move and the neighborhood crow crew is cawing back and forth talking about you. Little secret...we are. My advice? Sleep with one eye open.

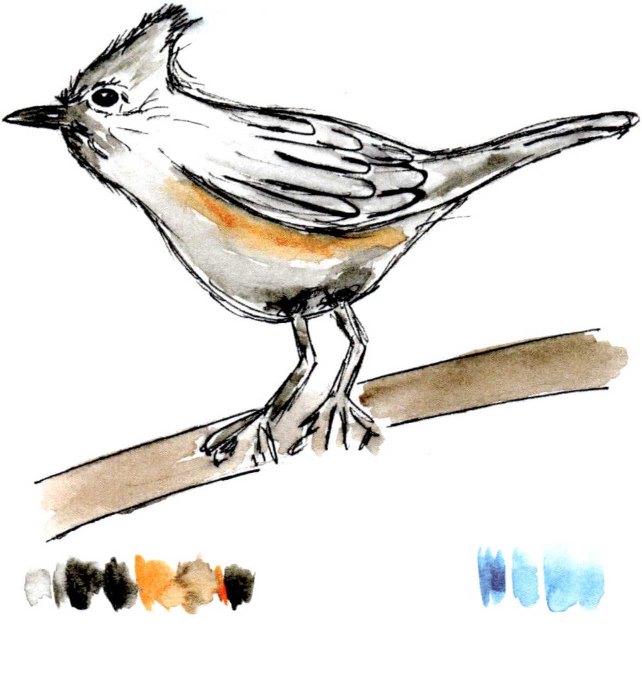

Dear Indoor Resident,

Seriously? Every time you say my name you're going to giggle? Greatly appreciated if you could conduct yourself more like an adult.

Affectionately,
The Tufted Titmouse

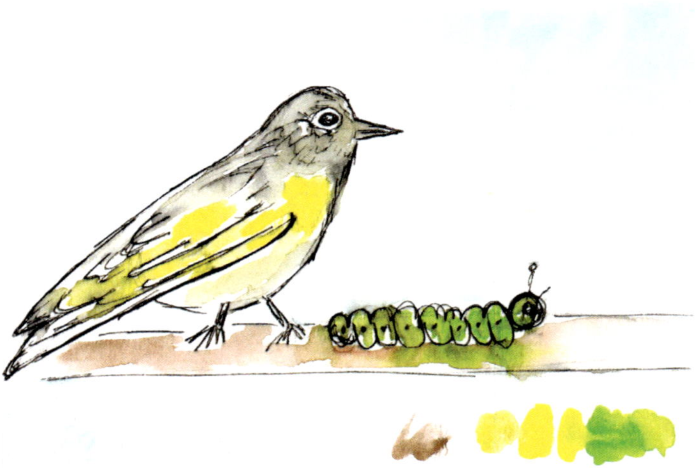

Unusual Friends

Somedays, you never know who you are going to sit next to.
If you do get to pick, pick kindly.
Pick someone you can lean your head on and laugh with.
Pick someone so different you might learn a thing or two.
Pick someone you don't want to snack on.

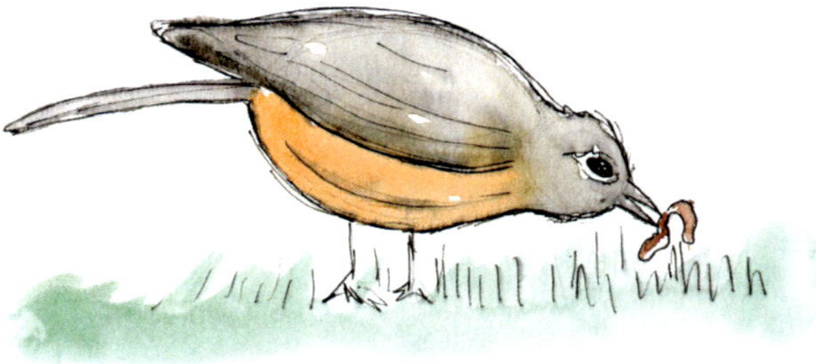

Honesty

girl to girl
honestly
tell me
does my butt look big when I bend over like this?

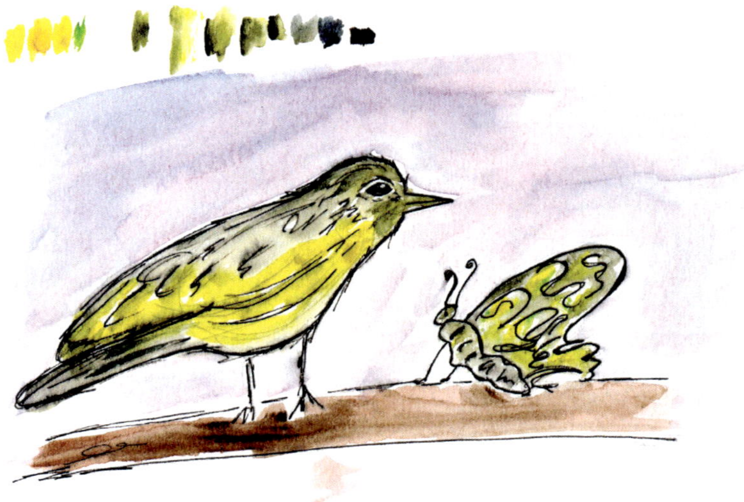

Unusual Friends (Part 2)

Something about you feels familiar. I think it's your eyes.
They smile when you look at me.
If I had arms, I would enjoy giving you a hug.
Are you sure we haven't met before?

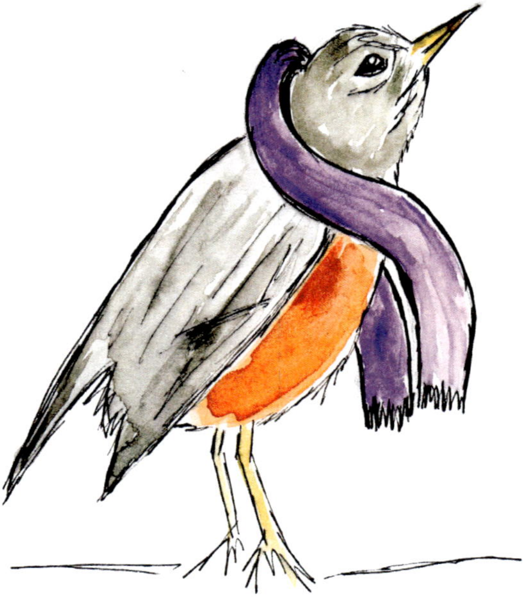

Choices

Today is April 19th and it's snowing. I'm cold and I'm trying not to regret my choice to be here.

I had other choices. Sunnier choices. Warmer choices. But I came back to South Street. I like your yard. You're usually pretty good about keeping the bird feeders full. The cats stay inside and don't try to kill me. All this gray though? It's hard to keep my head up. Thank goodness we have each other. At the end of the day, I suppose there is no other place I'd rather be than here, bundled up and waiting for the sun to shine with you.

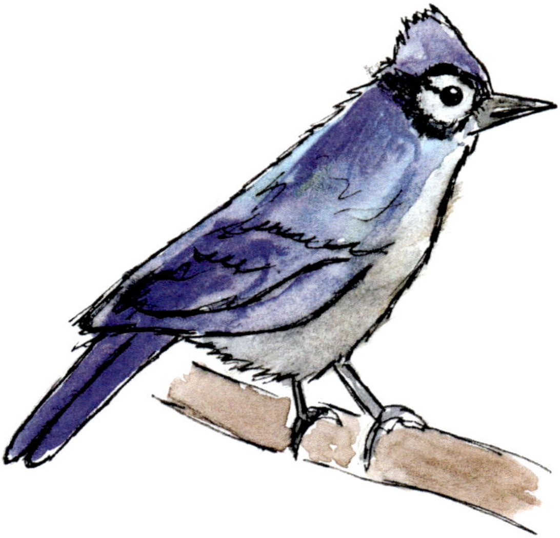

Bird Feeder Bully

I won't say his name out loud. Saying it out loud only makes him squawk louder, push his way thru the flock to gobble up all the sunflower seeds, fluff his chest feathers and peck at my head. So rude. Such a bully. He who shall not be named reminds me of one of your kind. I'll give you a hint who: Sometimes his tweets come out of the wrong end.
Rhymes with rump.

Affectionately,
The Chickadee

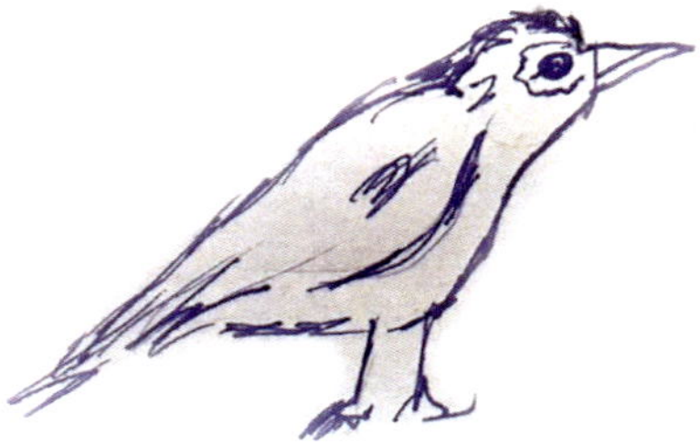

The Best We Can Do

What was that thing you found in your car while you were
looking for something to doodle on? I think it was a piece
of a peanut butter sandwich? Nutella? I don't know if
throwing it out the window was the right thing to do.
Is it safe to eat something unidentifiable? I knew one day
it would come to this, not wanting to miss a doodle day
and using an envelope and ballpoint pen in a parking lot.
Somedays, we just do the best we can.

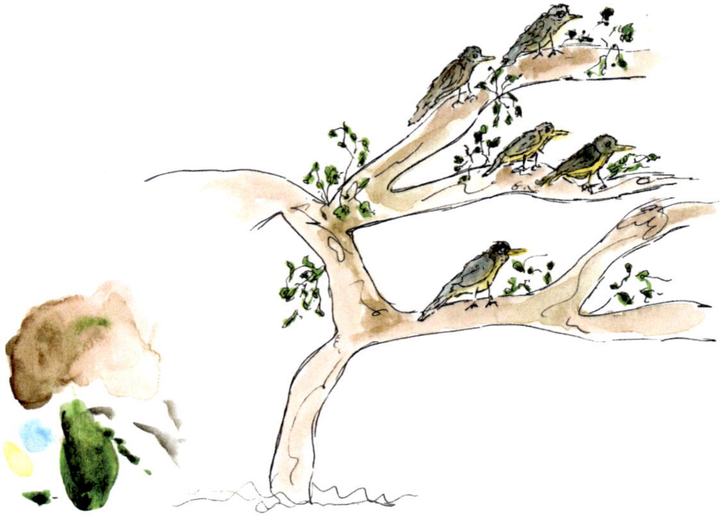

Marianne's Window

Keep your flock close.
They keep it real.
Celebrate sisterhood.

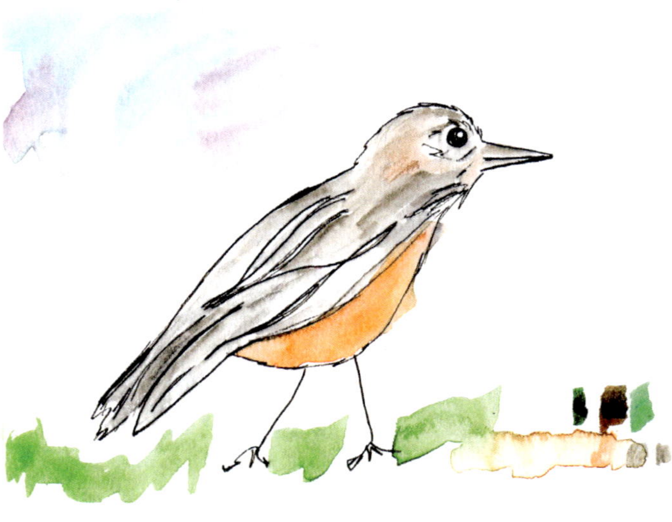

Central Park Robin

I'm not scared of that dog. Or the out-of-control kid racing toward me on a scooter. I am a city bird. Walk around me. I'm not moving. I own this park.

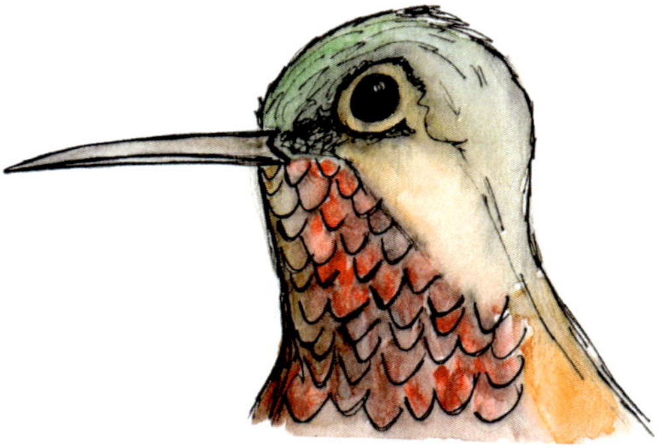

Frozen Hummingbird

Remember that time you found the dead hummingbird in your yard and you put him in the freezer? That was seriously weird. Maybe not as weird as when you drove around for 2 days with your frozen dead cat in your car, but still... very weird.

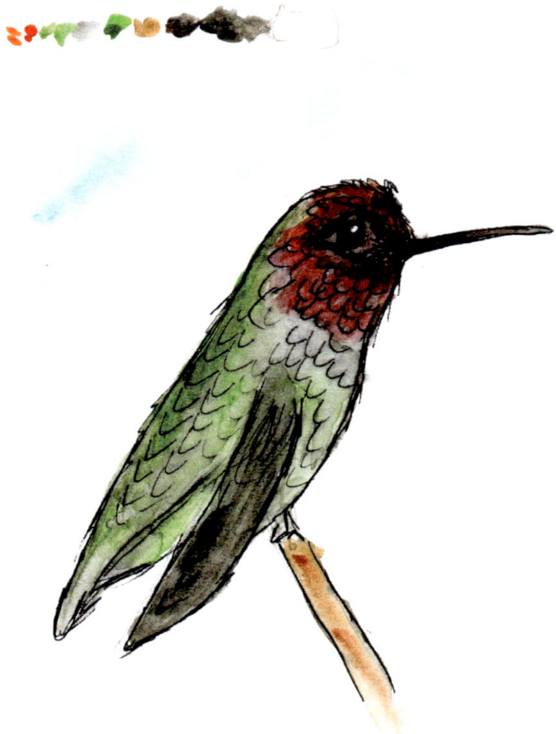

Art in the Park

I don't sit still for much. Quick bath. Quick trip to the feeder for some sugar. I just can't keep still. The one person I can sit still for is Art. He sits on the same bench at the same time every single day that it's not raining and has coffee and a muffin. He talks out loud to no one. I'm here listening. Hiding in the thick of this Azalea shrub. Listening to everything. For 45 years he has lived in this neighborhood. He used to have an act. He was a better dancer than a singer but was good enough to keep the show going for 30 years. He made most of his earnings betting at the race track. He knew when to stop for the day. That was the key to all his winnings, knowing when to walk away. The first year he started with the horses he was 22 years old and made 22,000 dollars. He never leaves the city. Why would he? Everything he needs is right here on the Upper East Side. Today he told no one except me listening from the bushes to stop eating romaine lettuce and to use more hand sanitizer. On your hands, not the lettuce. Just throw the lettuce away.
He's getting up.
Slowly.
Reaching for his cane.
Buttoning his coat.
It is 10:45 and it will take him 15 minutes to walk the few steps back to his apartment. He needs to be home at 11:00 for The Price is Right.
Game on.
Until tomorrow Art, game on.

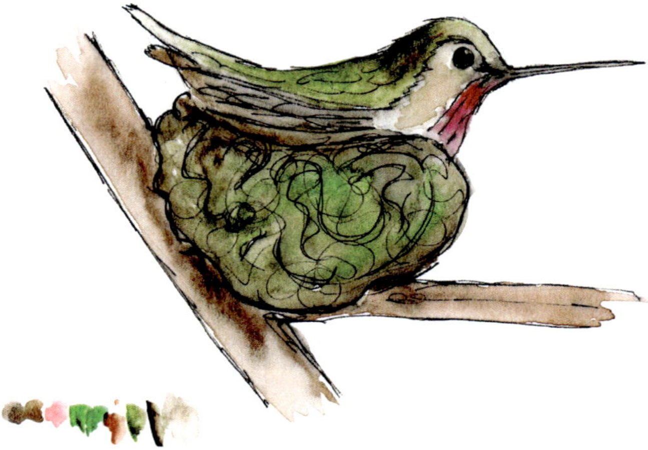

Hidden Nest

Keep looking.
Go ahead, look all day long.
Then look some more.
You're never going to find my nest.

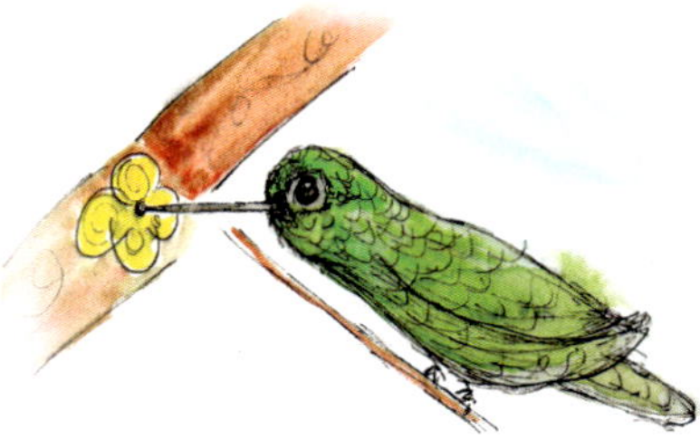

4 cups water
1 cup Sugar
for
Hummers

2 cups water
1/2 " Sugar

Food for Hummers

Nana didn't have to defend us from the cat like she did those slow-poke Chickadees. Not saying we didn't enjoy watching her take a broom to Sylvester the Cat. We did. Very much. "Less hunting, more swatting with the broom." That was our rallying cry for Parrish Lane. Oh and, more sugar please.

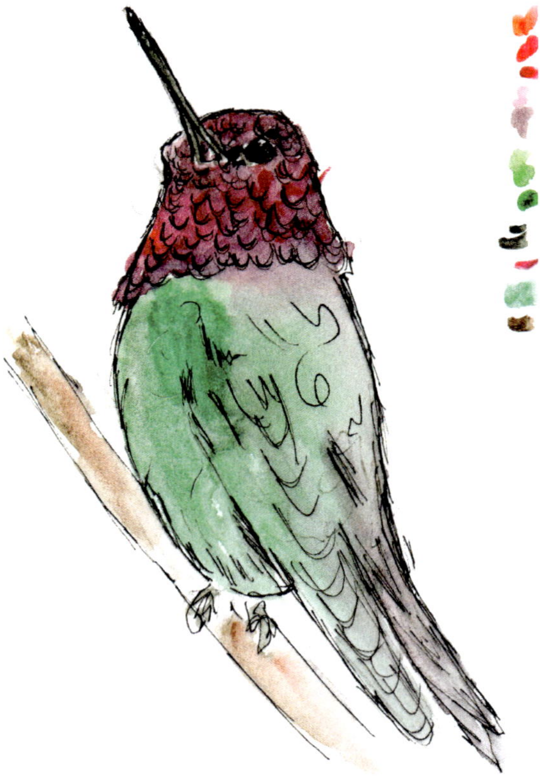

Rites of Spring

What you do for Spring:

- Make unrealistic lists of house projects that need to be done before summer. Realize they are unrealistic and rearrange the furniture and wash the windows instead.
- Cut a lot of your hair off for a new, lighter, summery look and deeply regret it 6 hours later.
- Also deeply regret all the Ben & Jerry's and Netflix that happened in February. Cross "get a new bathing suit" off your list and tell yourself the beach is not all that.
- Contemplate most recent relationship failure. Take very little responsibility for failure, consider match.com for 5 minutes. Watch dog videos instead.
- Spend your grocery money on Swedish clogs that are going to make your legs look long and lean despite the ice cream thing that happened in February. Love the clogs, the legs, eh, buy new flowy pants instead.
- Look at Pinterest gardening pages that offer suggestions for a border that will deter the 2 dozen new hoodlum bunnies in your backyard from eating your spring peas without hurting their feelings. Accept that there are no aesthetically pleasing fencing options and offer the peas to the bunnies as a sign of peace.

What I do for Spring:

- Show up and look pretty.

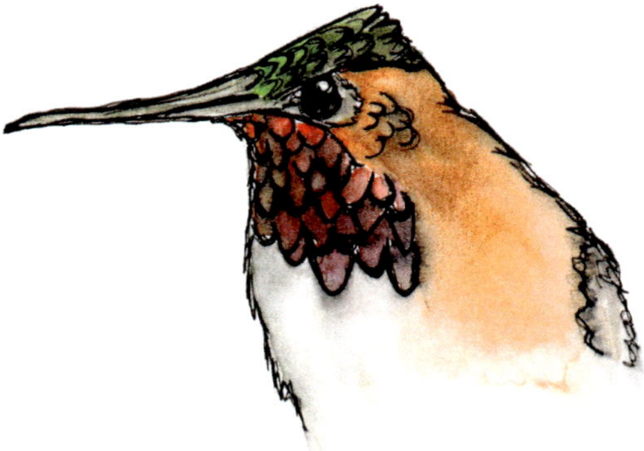

Humm on Mondays

It's just a Monday.
You've done thousands of Mondays.
Approximately two thousand four hundred
and ninety nine Mondays.
Pretty sure you can do this one too.
Find a smile.
Count your blessings.
Humm along to something snappy on the radio.
Put one foot in front of the other.
Get going.
Scoot.
Go.

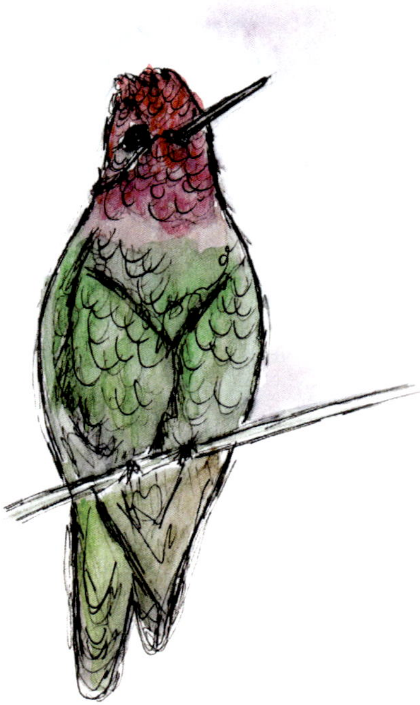

Philosophies

I know, you think my philosophies are simple.
Seize the day.
Find your smile.
Tweet like there is no tomorrow.
Show up and be pretty.
Yadda yadda, yadda.
My life expectancy is 5-7 years. Tops.
Monday, Sunday. They all need to be Fundays.
So yeah, find lots of things to smile about today.

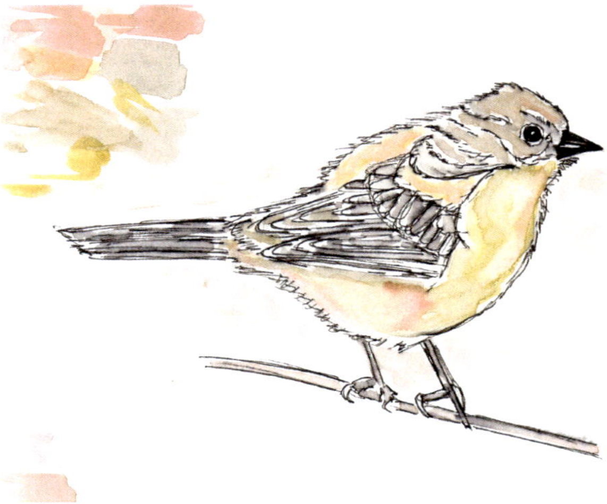

Reminders

Dang Girl.
I can see the claw marks you leave on the things you let go of.
Stop peeking behind you.
That's not the direction you're going.
Gets those wings flappin.
Forward, march.
Get going.
Scoot.
Go.

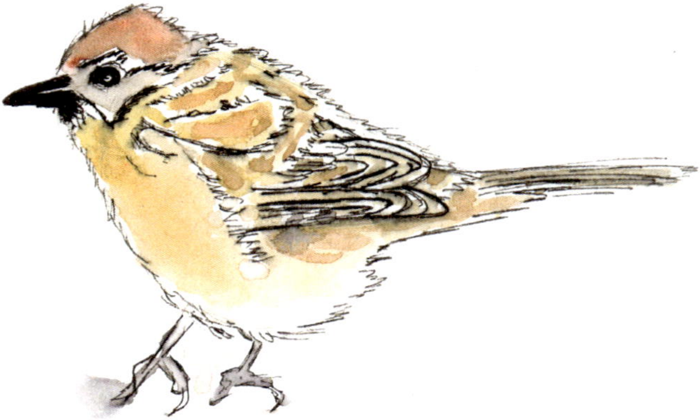

Book Club

Hey, what are you ladies doing in there?
Book club?
Wine club?
I see no books.
I see wine.
I see lots of snacks.
I hear a lot of laughing.
Still not seeing any books...
Best book club ever?
I want in.

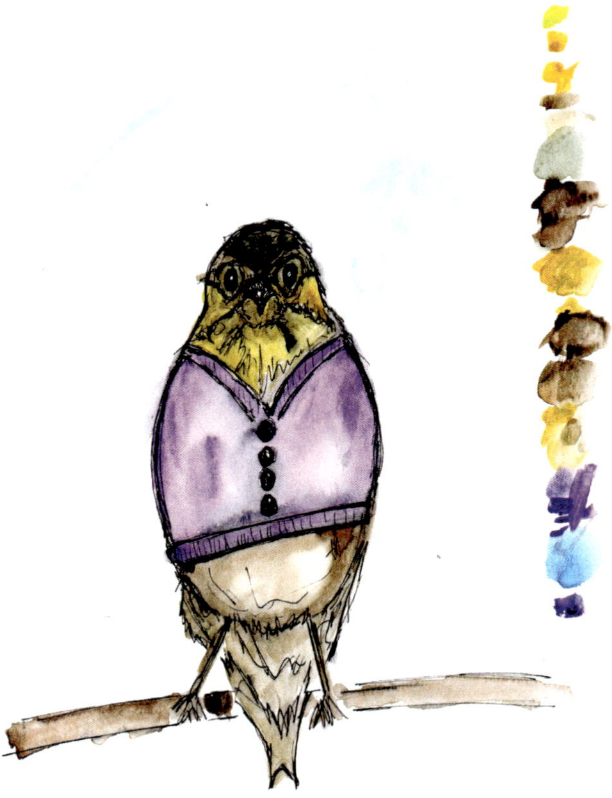

Sweater Vest
(5 days of reflections with Robert Frost)

"In 3 words I can sum up everything I've learned about life:
It goes on."
Robert Frost

"It goes on exceedingly better if you wear a sweater vest."
Kristina Henson

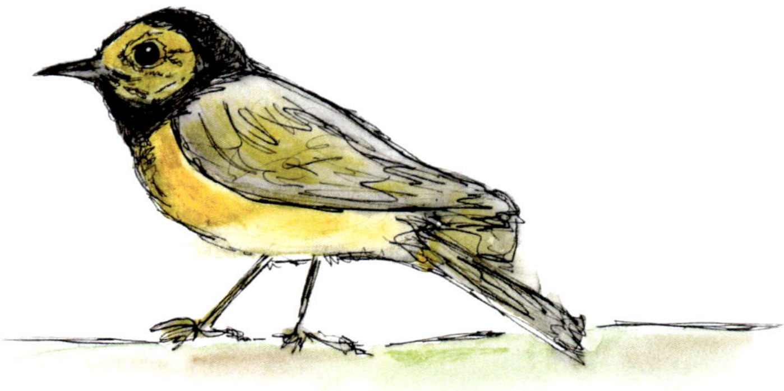

Lovesick
(5 days of reflections with Robert Frost)

"A poem begins as a lump in the throat, a sense of wrong, a homesickness, a lovesickness."
Robert Frost

"My lovesick poems are scribbled on paper that has been wrinkled by my tears."
Kristina Henson

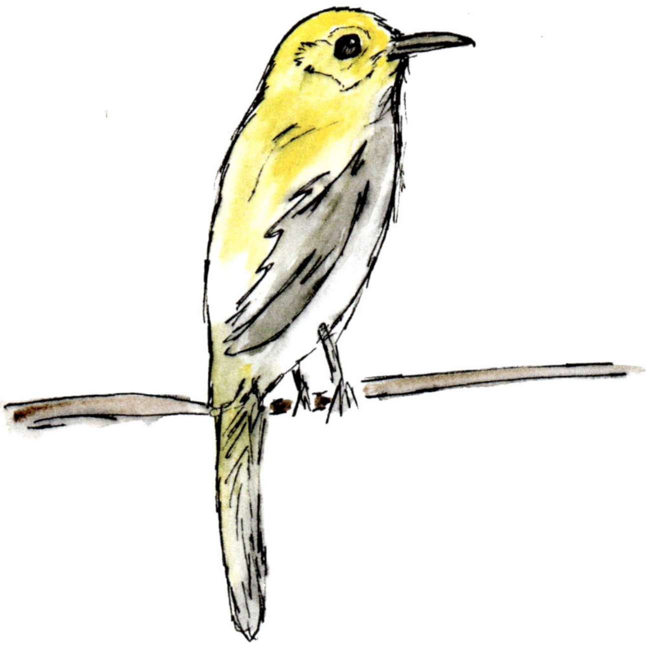

Irresistible Desire
(5 days of reflections with Robert Frost)

"Love is an irresistible desire to be irresistibly desired."
Robert Frost

"Sometimes, we make the irresistible desire to be loved way more complicated than it needs to be."
Kristina Henson

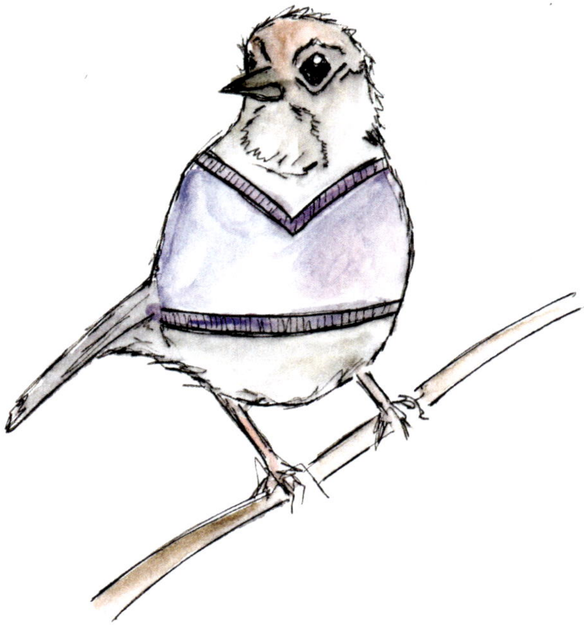

Clear the Fence
(5 days of reflections with Robert Frost)

"Don't ever take a fence down until you know why it was put up."
Robert Frost

"Don't jump over a fence unless you're fairly certain you can clear it."
Kristina Henson

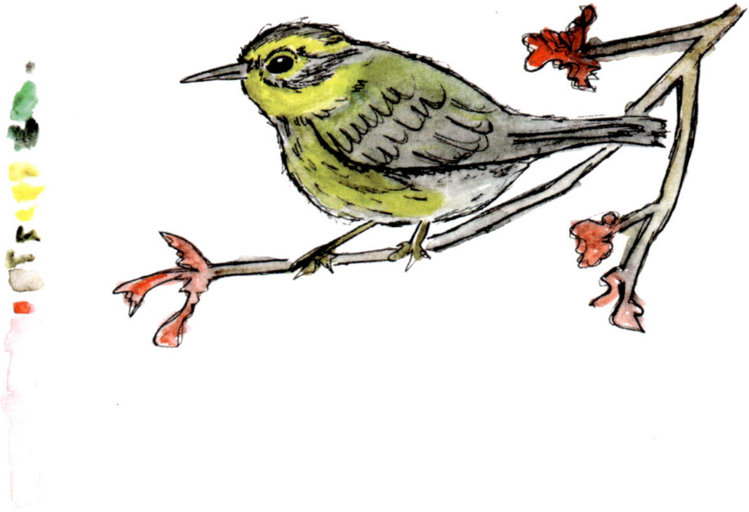

Swarming
(5 days of reflections with Robert Frost)

"These woods are lovely, dark and deep."
Robert Frost

"These woods are swarming with black flies
and I cannot run."
Kristina Henson

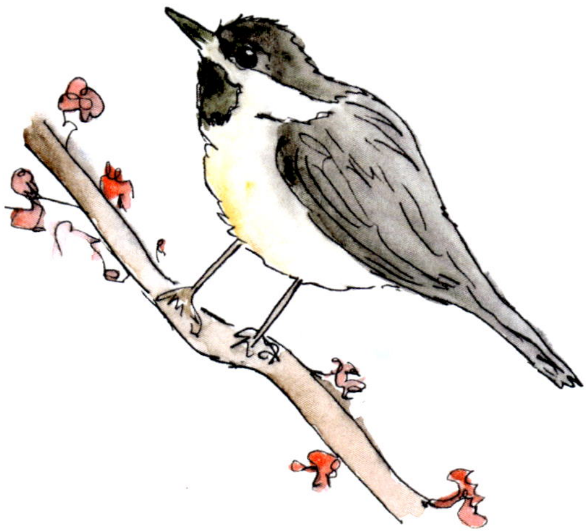

Feed Me

You spent 10 minutes this morning helping the bumble bee who was frantically banging his little bee body against the window to find his way back outside. It was kind of you to save the fool who flew into the house by choice. In my opinion, it could have been time better spent. Like maybe filling up the bird feeders before you peeled out of the driveway so you wouldn't be late for work? That screaming you heard? That was me. God help me, I hope I don't faint. Hurry home. Feed me.

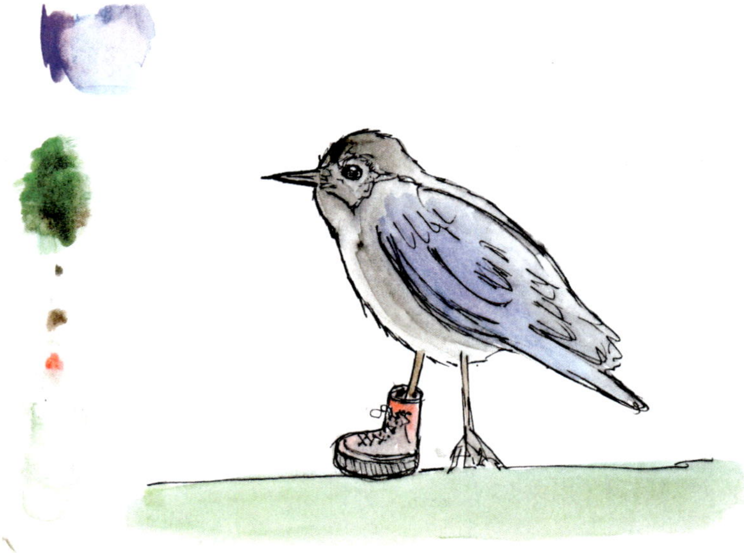

Barbie Shoe

I can explain the Barbie shoe. You know, it's one of those
things you wonder about. Can I pull off a hightop platform
sneaker with these legs? It was just there. Sticking out of the
mud by the swings at the park. Just my size. Or so I thought.
I tried it on, gazed at my reflection in a puddle and laughed
out loud at how ridiculous I looked. Now, it's a bit too snug.
I can't shake it off. Help a sister out. I'll sit. You pull.
We can pretend this never happened.

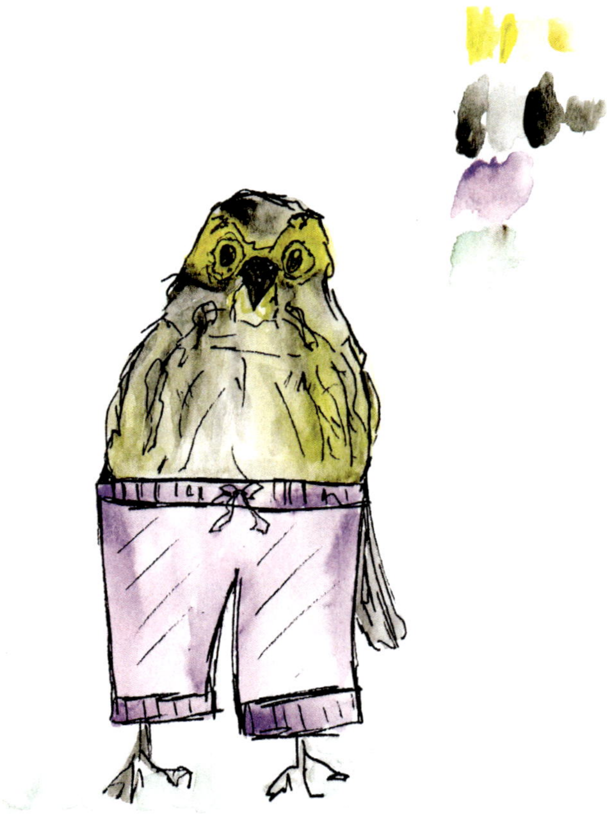

Friday Nights

Purple pajama bottoms.
Popcorn.
Precious Pearl.
Pretty picture books.
Pleasant dreams.

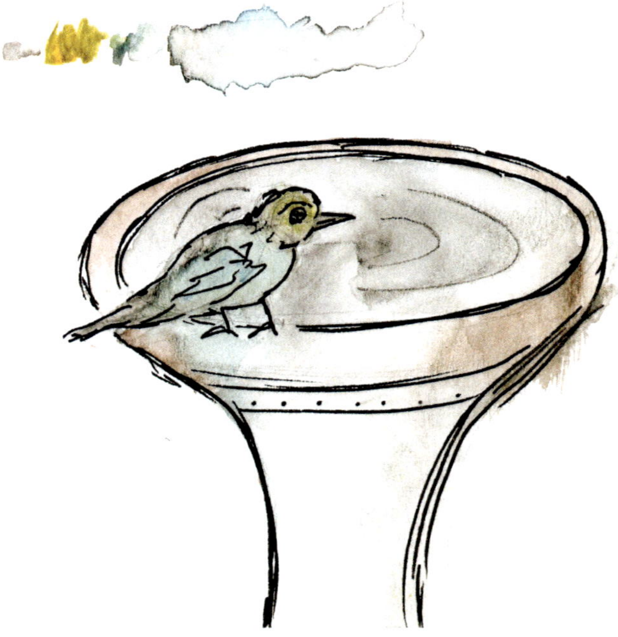

Bird Bath

I like the bird bath.
You like the gong bath.
To each his own.

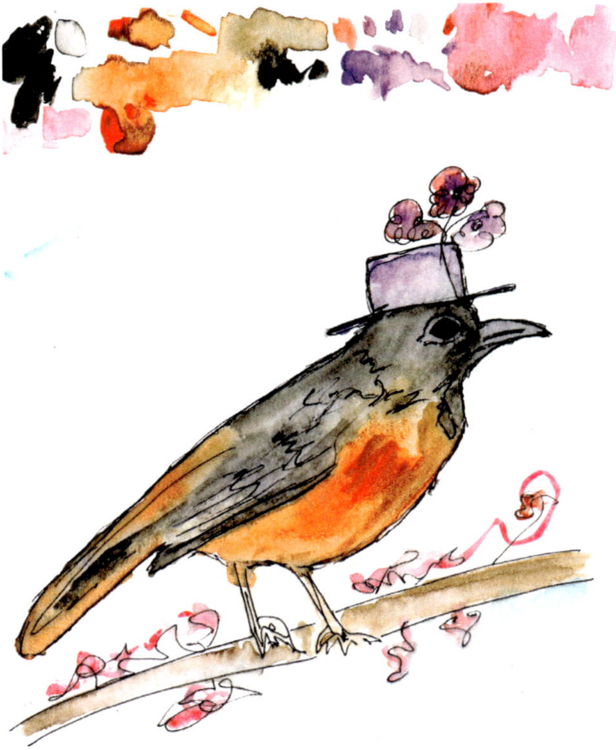

Mother's Day

Sometimes, I wake up and I'm still tired.
I go to work. I cook. I clean. I pick up all the dog poop from
the yard and really don't mind even though she swore she
would always do it. I love her. I love the dog.
I laugh. Often. At myself. At us. At the world.
I apply band-aids.
I comb out tangles.
I feel the greatest joy just by looking at her. Hearing her voice.
I worry.
I wish she would eat more green vegetables.
I wish she wouldn't roll her eyes so much.
I wish she wouldn't slam her bedroom door.
I am happy to be a Mother.
I am happy to be her Mother.

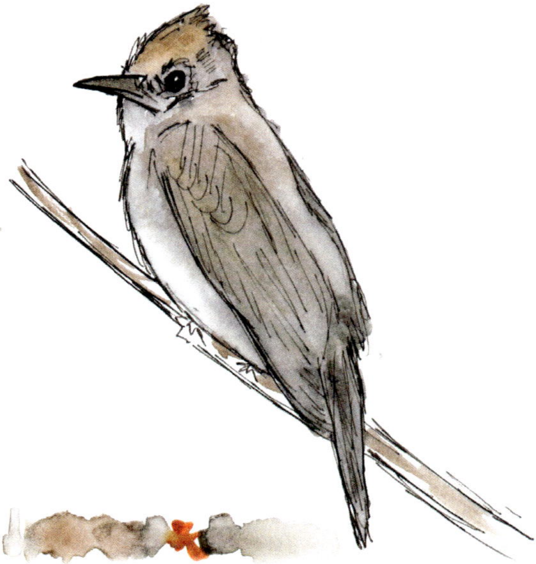

Dandelion

I have a secret. I love Dandelions. I know, people spend a lot of time and a small TruGreen fortune to get rid of them. I think they're pretty. It's gorgeous to fly over a field bursting with yellow. Sunflowers shouldn't get all the golden glory. I'll shout it from this treetop,
"I love you Dandelion. You're not just a weed!"

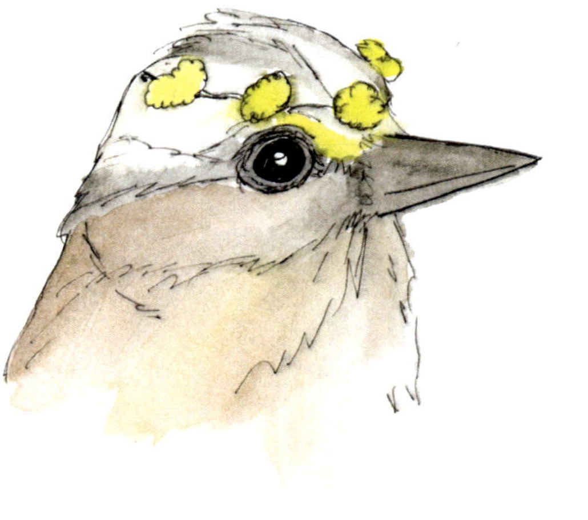

Crown of Dandelion

Another thing about Dandelions, you can tie them together and make a crown. I'm wearing this until Saturday. Just in case Prince Harry comes to his senses and realizes that I am the girl of his dreams. I was born to be a Princess.
And I have this crown.

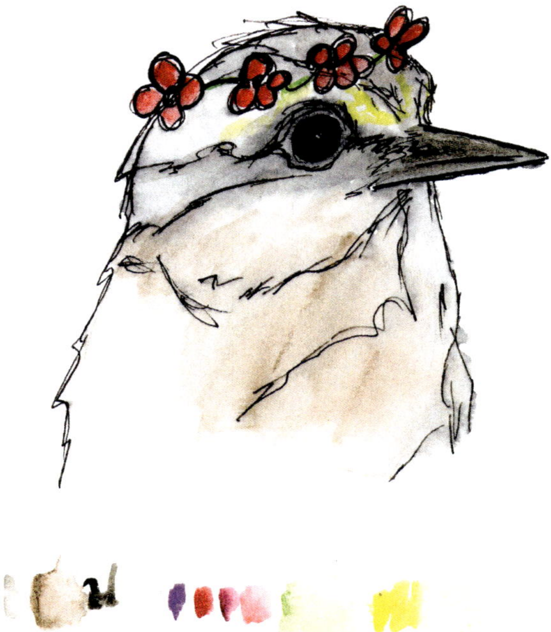

Princess Chickadee

The Dandelions went limp and lost their oomph.
Day Two of wearing a crown in anticipation of becoming
Princess Chickadee Sparkle Pants Elizabeth Louise Windsor.

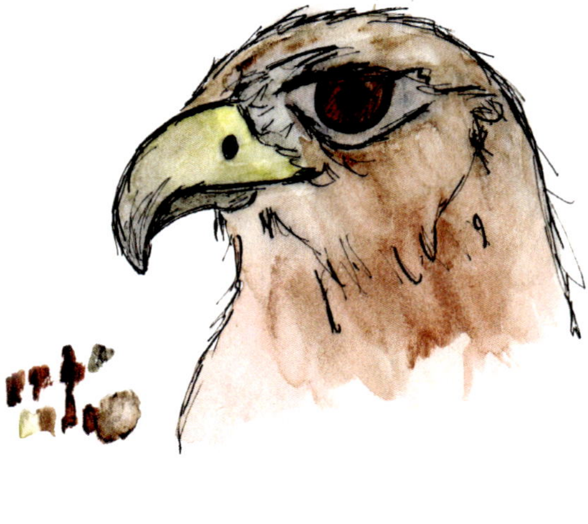

I Pray

I pray.
To whom or to what I do not know for sure.
I'm sure someone is hearing the constant chatter in my head.
Something bigger than me.
My prayers get answered.
See that mouse?
I prey.

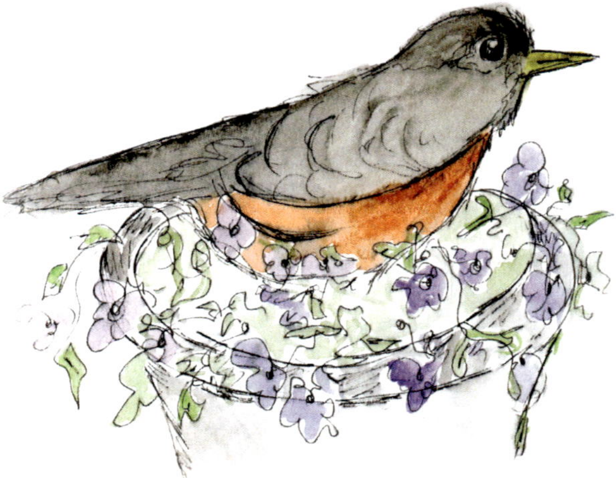

Differences

The differences between your Grandmothers is a hoot.
Nana, the Irish, nurtured us and sang like a songbird.
Nunny, the Italian, just threw a slipper at me for
sitting in her pot of pansies.

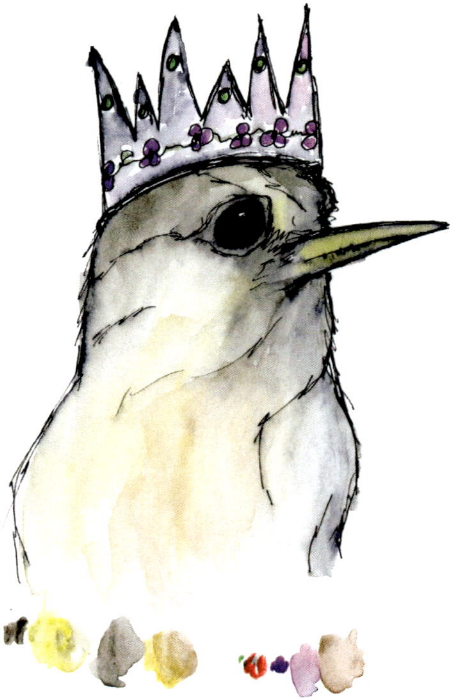

Harry Is Married

So, no Harry. It's ok. I am still full of hope
and love. Here, I shall maintain my post, as Queen
of this charming little house on South Street.

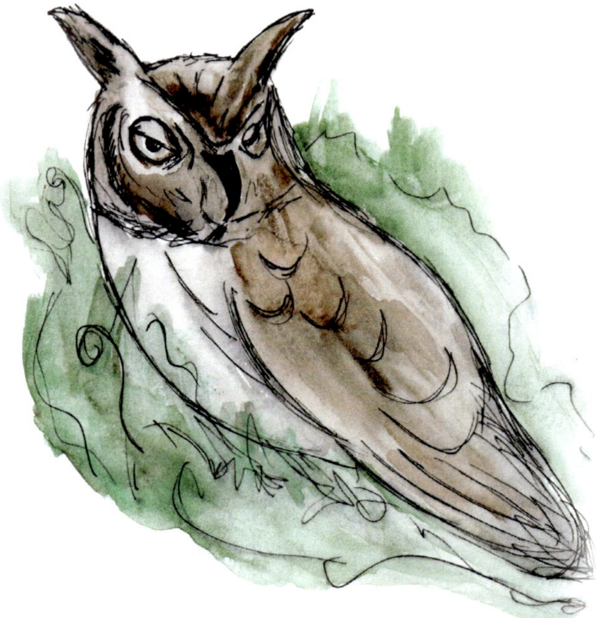

A Mouse

That mouse
In the house
You think he's a louse?
What about this fat
Rat
As large as your cat
I have already eyed
There is nowhere to hide
I'm glad he's outside
He might be my dinner
Again, I'm the winner

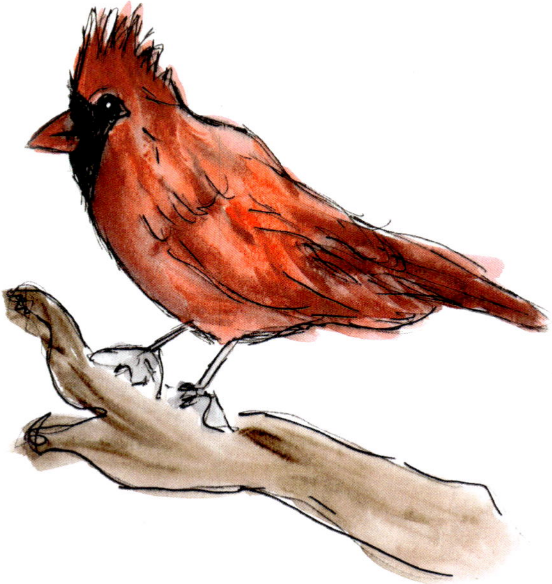

Defining Your Space

I am marking my territory with this beautiful song.
This, my friend, is much classier than that dog
of yours peeing on the neighbor's shrubs.

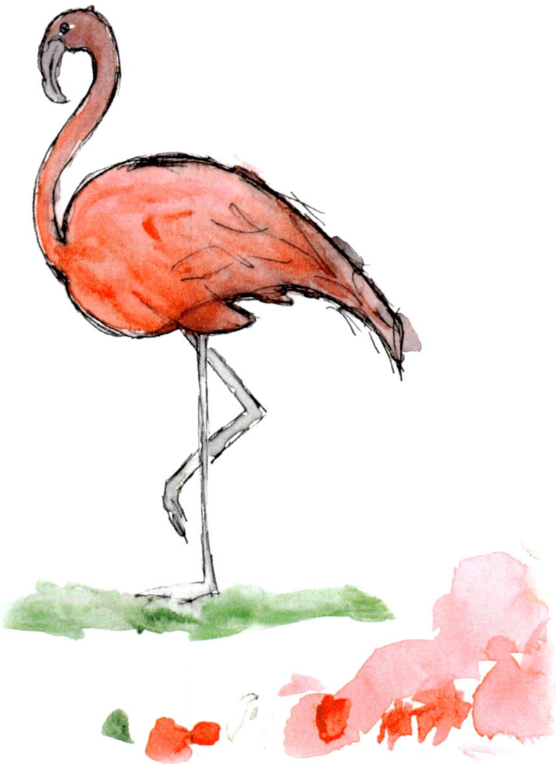

Flamingo Relationships

The divorce rate among Flamingos is 99%.
How can we take matters of the heart
seriously when we look like this?
I'm pink.
Leggy.
And perhaps a little too eager to Tango.

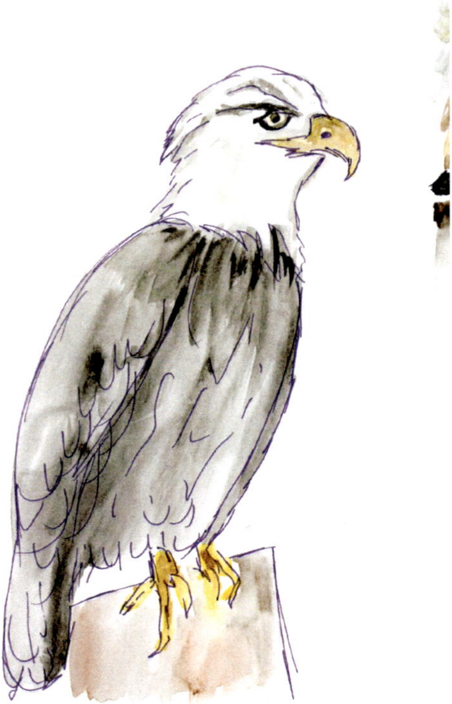

Independence

It was her independence
and strength
that made me fall in love with her.
She's fierce.
I'm with her until death parts us.

As the years pass, it's her independence
and strength
that scares me too much to ever leave.

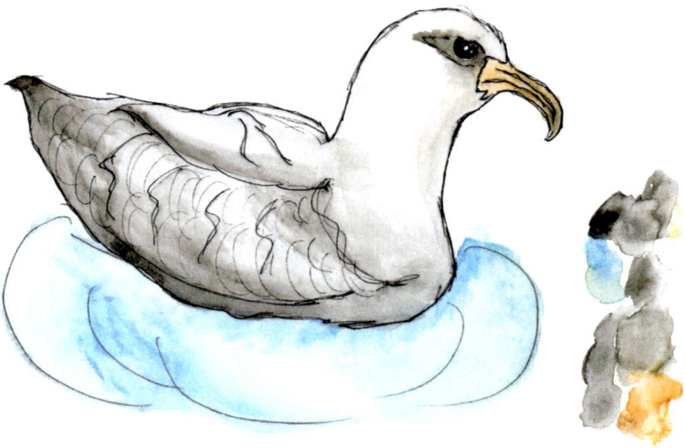

The Albatross

It took me years and a lot of dramatic dancing to find him. Only to him do I pledge my undying love and devotion. 80% of my life is spent out at sea. Alone. Maybe that is what keeps our relationship strong. Not seeing each other for months and years at a time makes getting under each other's skin practically impossible. When the time is right, I know when and where to find him. It's a mystery to us too. This devotion to only each other. For all of my life, I will always find my way back to him. The Albatross.

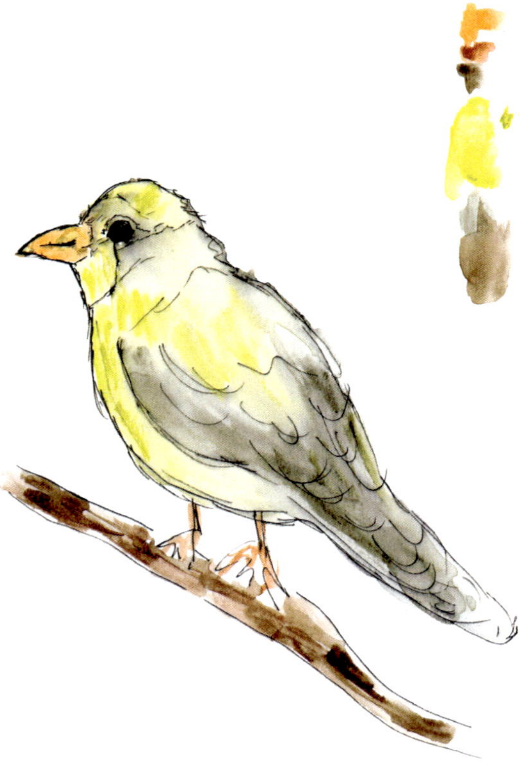

Replay

Sometimes, when he is telling you a story about his past, he closes his eyes. Is he watching the replay on the screen in his mind's eye? Is he concentrating really hard to remember the details? Or, is he trying to avoid looking at the salad dressing that dribbled down your shirt?

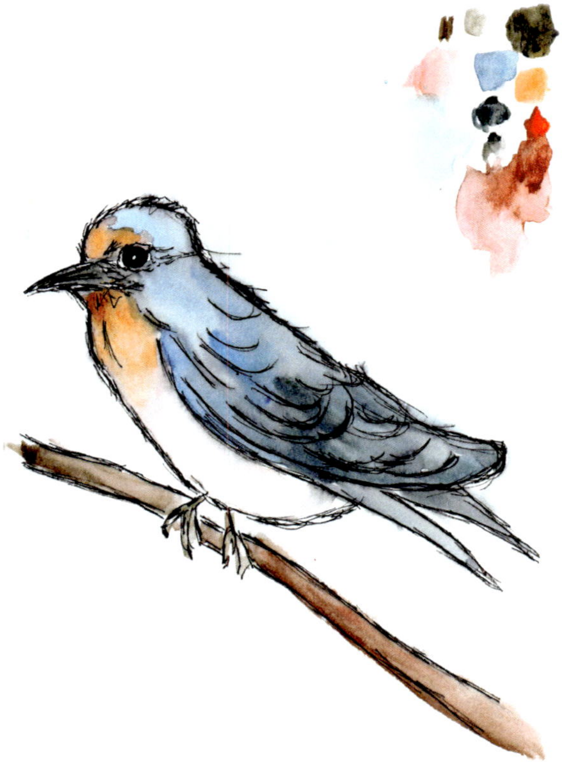

Barn Swallow Farmer

If we get to pick our next lives, I want to be a farmer.
I want to plow fields in a red tractor. I'm going to listen
to Johnny Cash, drink a cold can of PBR and watch the
sun set as I leave tidy rows of overturned earth behind me.
In my next life, I'm getting out of the Barn Swallow
business. I'm going to be a farmer.

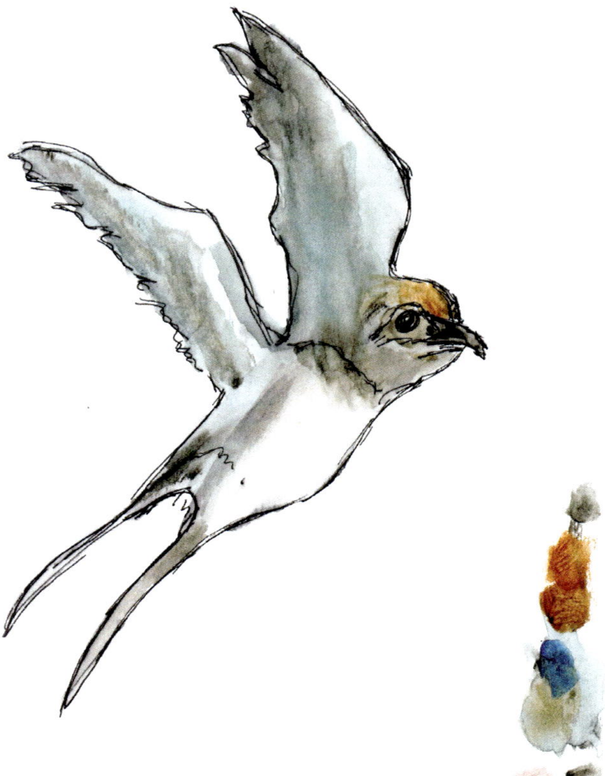

Naked Farming

Once in a while I see this farmer out driving his tractor with no shirt on. I can only see him from the waist up and I can't help but wonder if he has pants on. Is naked farming a thing? When I'm a farmer, I am always going to wear a shirt.
And pants. At the same time.

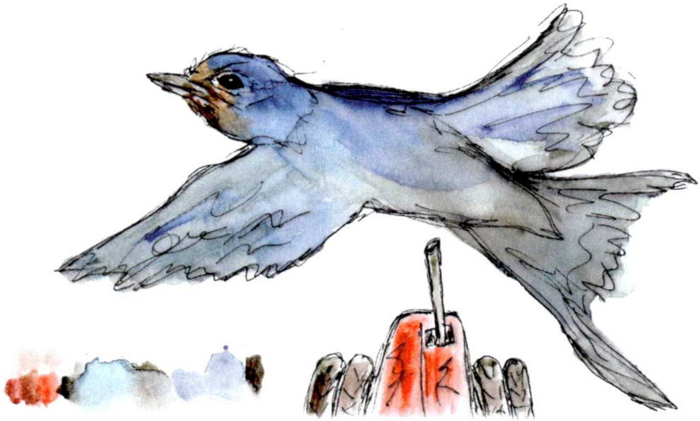

Church is Optional

Going to church will be optional on Sundays when I'm farming. Being out in a field, behind the wheel of my red Massey Ferguson planting vegetables is as close to God as I'm ever going to get.

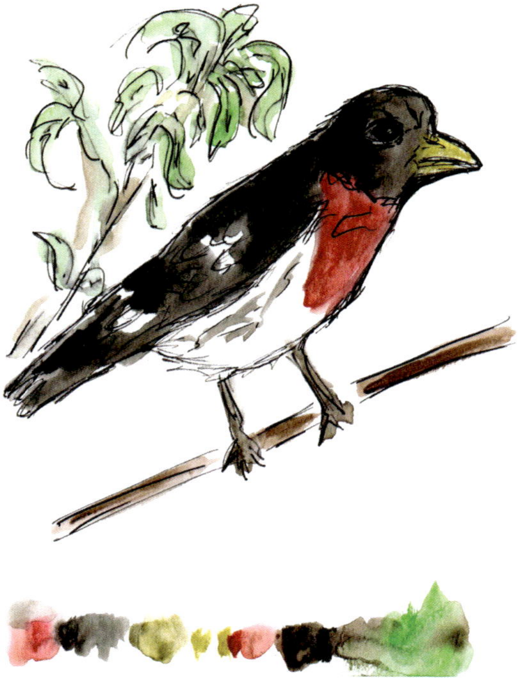

Be Still

Sit still more often and listen to us sing.
Just sit there.
Close your eyes.
Be still.
Turn that phone off.
All that noise in your head,
the cars passing,
dogs barking,
kids laughing,
when that all becomes the background
you can really hear us sing.
We have so many different songs.
From time to time, you forget to listen.

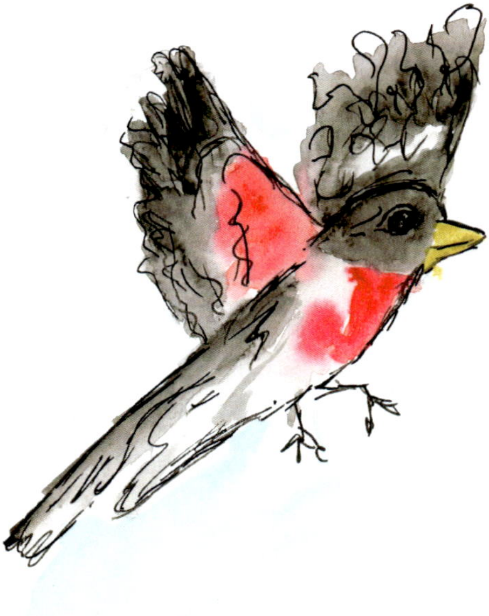

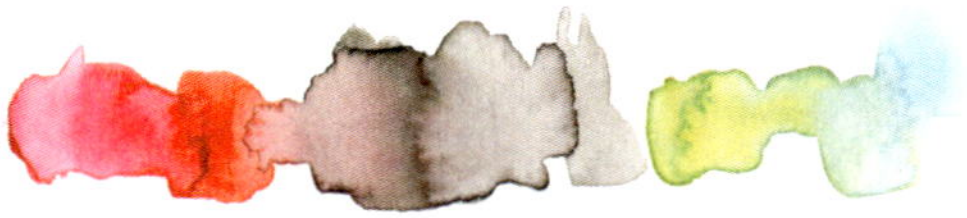

Perched

I flew in quietly and perched on a horse. I don't think he knew I was there. Earlier in the day, I witnessed quite a ghastly scene when the crinkling of a plastic bag terrified him. I can't imagine he would be calm, cool and collected knowing he had a hitchhiker on his rump. This spot on his butt is warm from the sun. It's my favorite place to sit still and think.

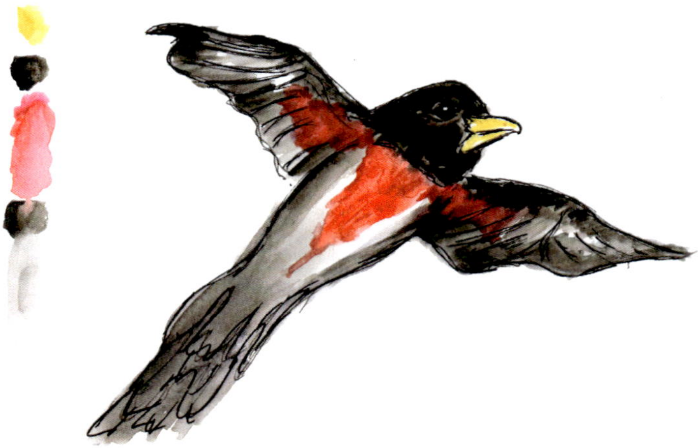

Backyard Beatle

Yes, birds can meditate. Where do you think The Beatles and Maharishi got their inspiration from? That's right. A bird. I'm like the George Harrison of your backyard. Maybe I'm not as sexy as him but I definitely got a little bit of a hipster swagger going on. I could totally rock a man-bun if I wanted to. I am a trendsetter.

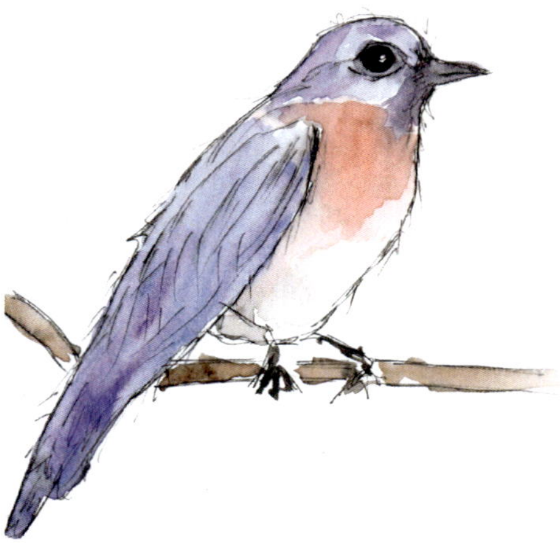

Kookey

I know you have concerns about becoming a kooky not so young person that lives alone with a flock of freeloading stray animals. Just a little tip? Maybe you wouldn't look so kooky if you stopped puttering around the yard talking to your vegetable plants and random insects. Pretty sure your neighbors were watching you today. I don't know. It's just a suggestion.

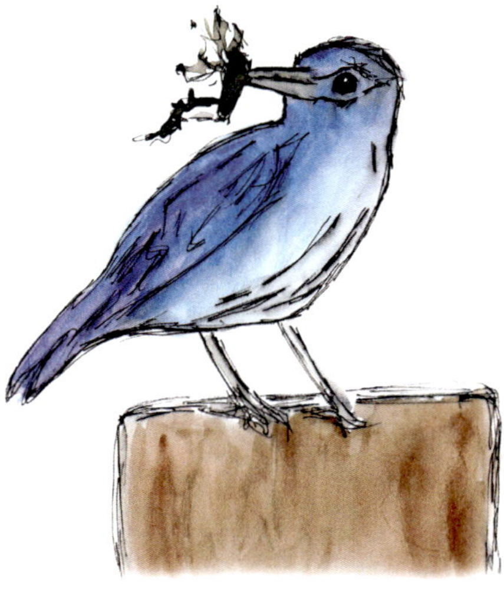

Dinner

Nom nom nom...
There is now one less cricket for you to chit chat with.

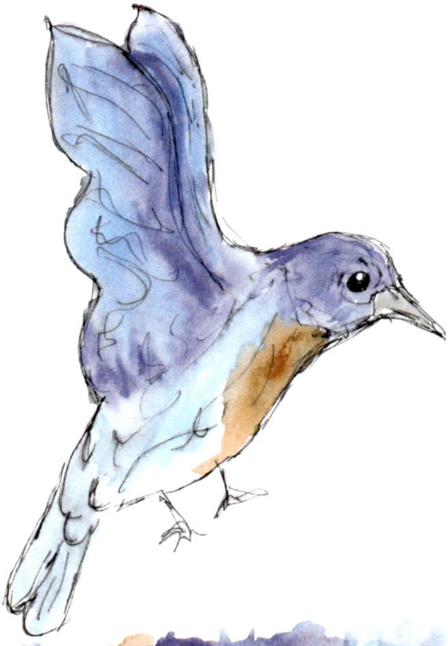

Parade Day

How sweet it is to sit in your front yard with the people
you love the most in the whole world and watch a parade
march by. The only thing I would change, if I could,
would be throwing sunflower seeds instead of candy.
I'm pretty much always thinking about my next snack.

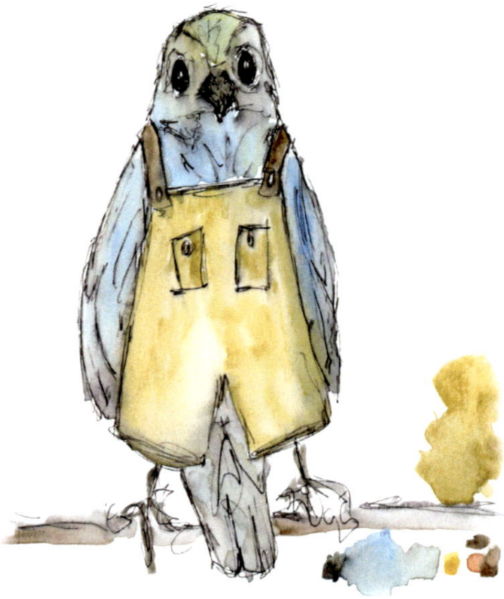

Birds Wearing Clothes

Thanks for the Carhartts. I watched one episode of Naked and Afraid and feel so vulnerable. Damn that man for bending over to build a camp fire.

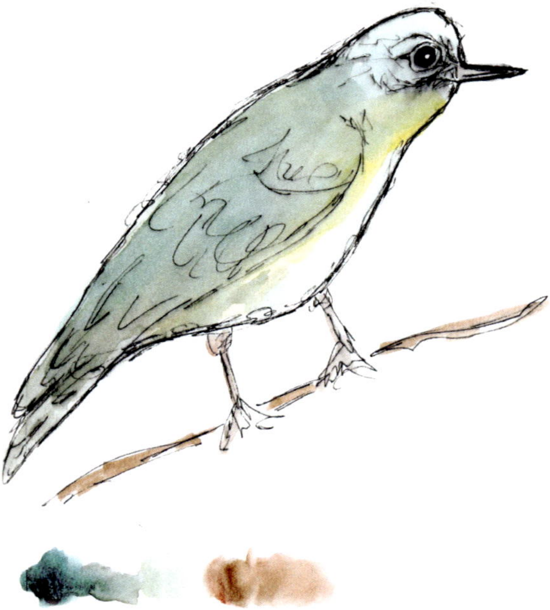

Vulnerabilities

In addition to showing up with no pants on, singing in public also makes me feel vulnerable. It's too bad. It crushes my rock star fantasy. I'm fine when it's just us in our own yard. Get me in front of a flock, I'll just about faint if you ask me to sing. Just put a bag over my head so I can't see anyone looking at me. Then I'll carry on like a canary.

All that is baby stuff compared to being in love. Nothing feels more vulnerable than that.

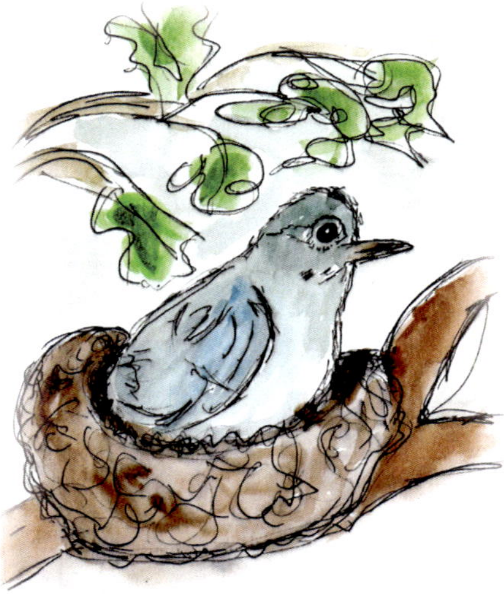

Rain

the rain
is dripping on my head
drip
drip
drip
it's making me sleepy
my eyes are closing
you're in the house
listening
it's peaceful, the dripping
we both feel the same way
grateful for a place
to call home
when it's raining

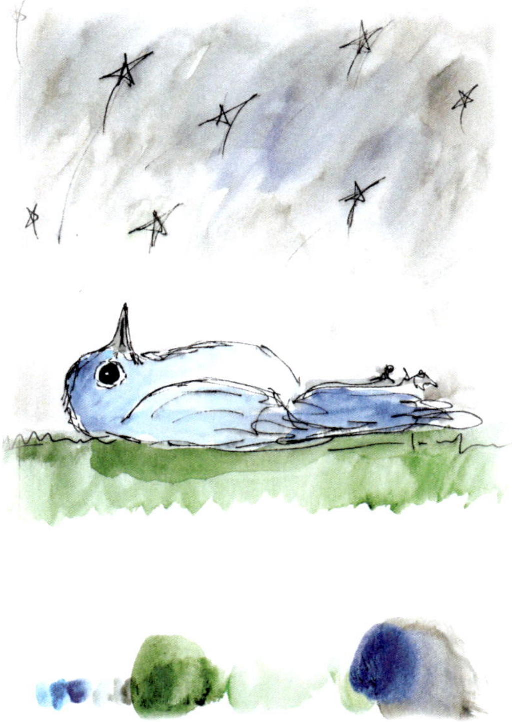

Under the Stars

I got the best ideas for figuring out my sticky
situations while lying here under the stars.
I didn't need my therapist.
I just needed the day to end.

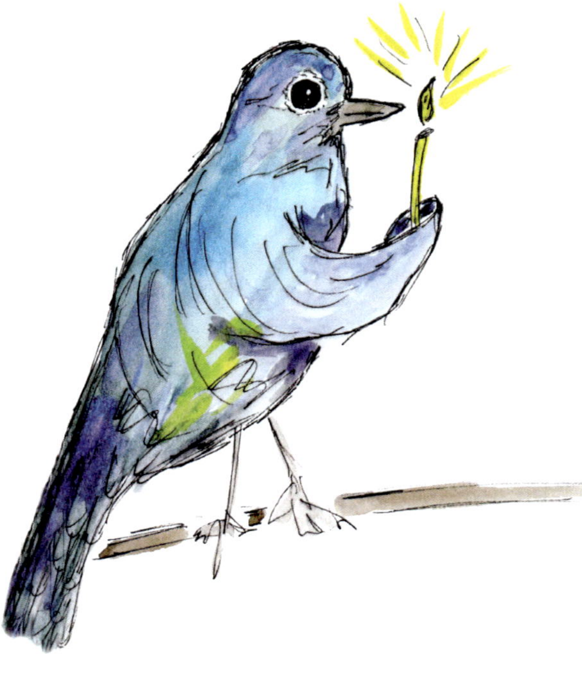

A Little Light

When I hear creepy noises, I have to
remind myself not to be afraid in the dark.
For all my days on this earth so far,
the sun has never failed to show up.
I can always find a little light.
I'm one of the lucky ones.

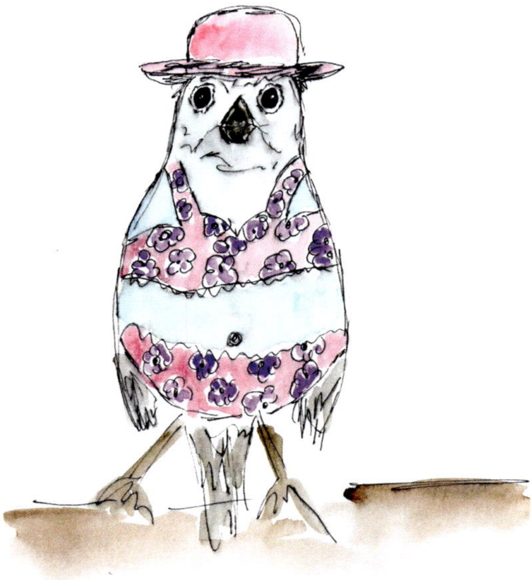

I Love Bread

I do not accept bread to be the Antichrist. So please, keep throwing your toast crumbs by the bird feeder. I've wiggled into this bikini and my squishy bits and I will be at the bird bath soaking up the sun and thanking God for putting wheat on the menu.

P.S. A little speck of blueberry jam would also be ok.

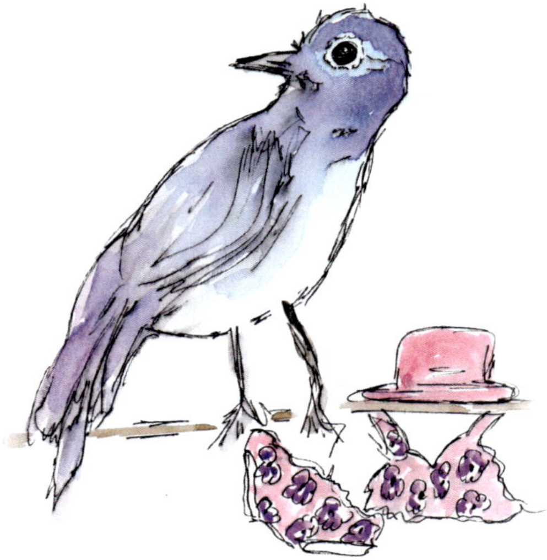

(Later at the Bird Bath)

Did you see what he did?
The Blue Jay!
That loud mouth know-it-all show-off.
He took my pink hat.
Him and that crow played frisbee with it.
He splashed all around.
Made a mess.
Ate my snack.
Then flew away screeching like a madman.
Wait.
Do you think he has a crush on me?
Is being a jerk a new mating ritual?
I'm hanging my suit out to dry.
This is all too confusing and scary.

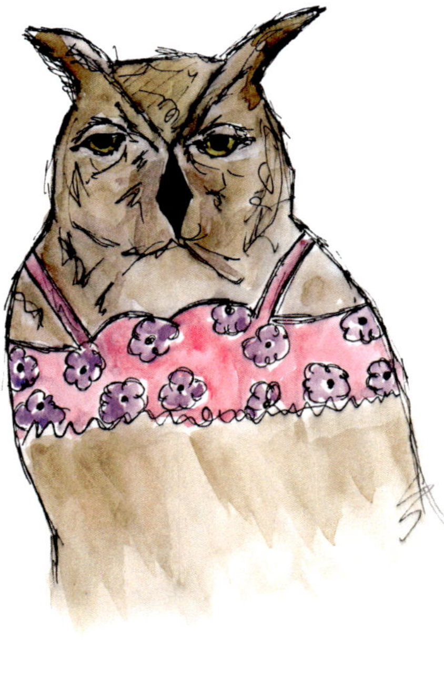

Wise Friends

Oh sweet Blue Bird. Trust your wise old friend on this one. Jerks have been making messes and screeching since the beginning of time. They kind of have to get sprinkled into the mix. It helps the good ones to really sparkle. Oh. This bikini top? It was just hanging from a tree branch.
I love me in pink.

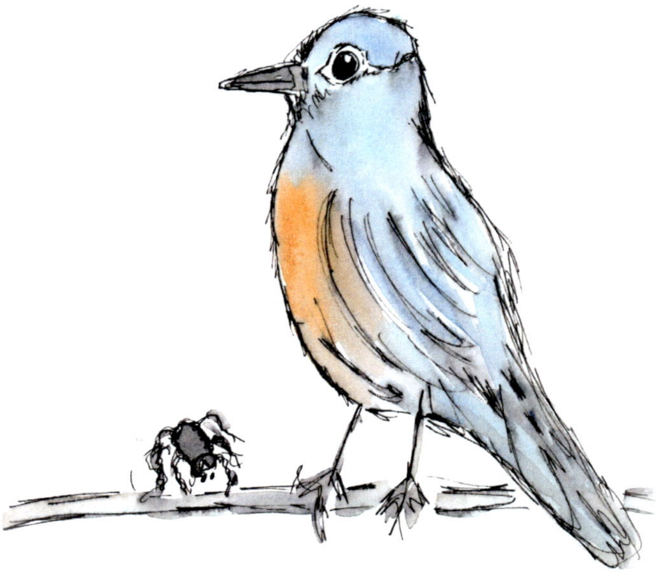

The Jumping Spider

I'm not very picky about my insect snacks. I do however
draw the line with that jumping spider. This is exactly why
you're on your own with that giant one on the hose spigot.
You, staring wide eyed, back and forth between me
and the spider is in no way luring me to eat him so
you can turn the hose off.
This is your big plan?
Someone has to eat the spider?
One of us has to make a move. I'm betting it's going to be
you. I can sit here all night. You will eventually whine for your
pajamas and need to turn the hose off before the basement
floods. Funny, where is that idiot Blue Jay when we need him?
He'd probably eat it.
Why, God?
Why does he need to have the ability to lunge himself at me
from a mile away with those gigantic beady eyes?
Why the jumping spider?
I have so many questions.

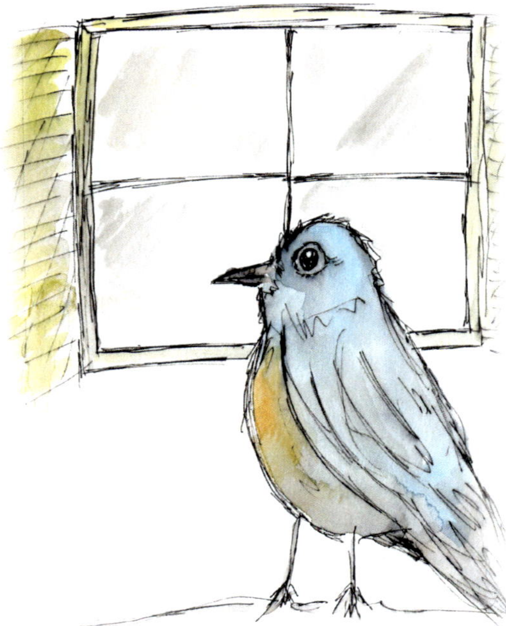

God, since I have your ear about the jumping spider, I have another question. Do you get mad at me when I swear and use your name? For the record, I'm legitimately trying to quit swearing but it's not going so great. That time when I flew into the window really hard and almost broke my beak off, I yelled God damn it after I regained consciousness and shook it off. I didn't mean to dishonor you. With the utmost respect, I really truly did want you to damn that window. You're not too mad?

I'm just a bird; my overall level of sinning feels pretty small.

Ok, ok, I'll try harder to stop swearing.

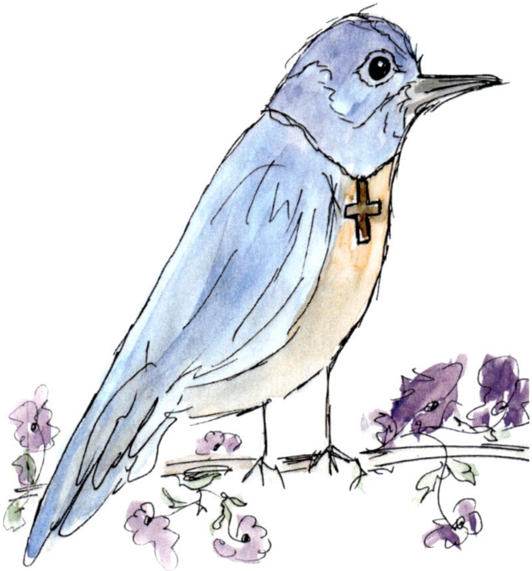

J.C.

Jesus Christ.
These are two more words that are frequently flying out of this beak. Like yesterday, when someone flew right in front of me and cut me off, I chirp screeched, "Jesus Christ, did you see that guy?" It's more like we are having an ongoing conversation rather than I'm constantly being disrespectful. You're one guy I really like. I'm pretty sure you never would have stolen my pink hat and played frisbee with it with one of your Apostles. I don't know what heaven is like but if you ever get annoyed in the spirit world, it would be okay with me if you muttered *Blue Bird* under your breath.
You probably don't get too annoyed though do you?
Because, like, you're Jesus.
But if you need to, I'd be honored.
Peace out J.C.

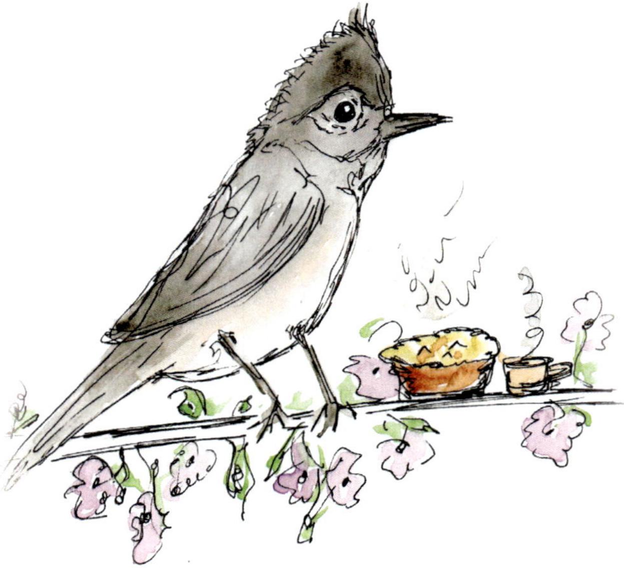

I Like Pie

Please tell me why
it's so hard to fly
with a belly all full
of strawberry pie

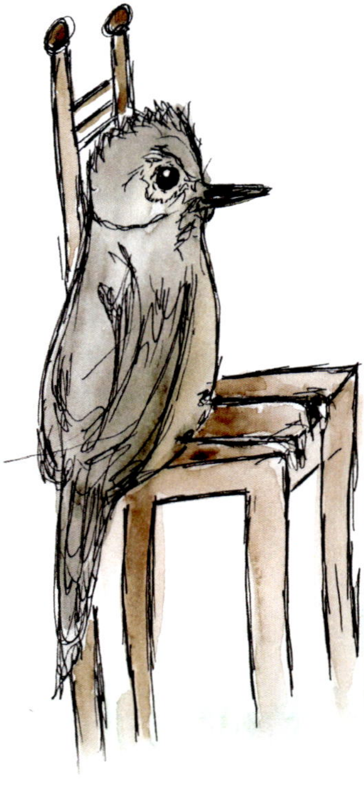

Solo Flight

I have flown
Alone
To destinations unknown
Once there
Without a care
I just sit, and stare
You should try this sometime
While you're still in your prime
You could sit in this chair and continue my rhyme

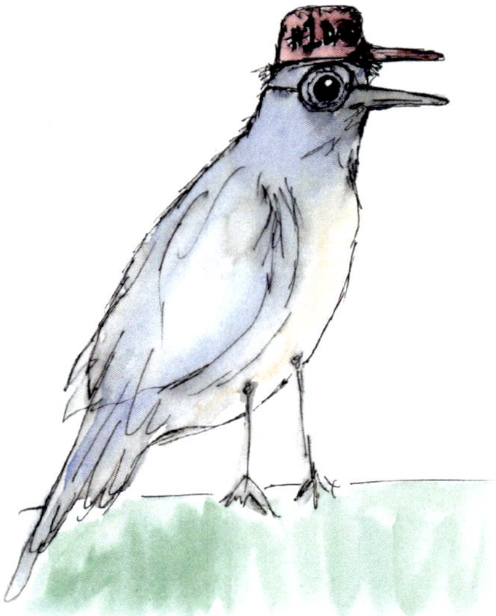

Dave

I've noticed your eyes are the same shape.
The same color.
He's 73. You're 49.
Wow. You've known each other a long time.
He's a master tool and die maker.
He likes car racing.
His dog.
The Erie Canal.
Fishing on the lake.
His kids.
Trains going by and things with loud motors make him happy.
For such a dude, he never seems to mind that he never
had a son. He learned a lot about nail polish and girl drama.
You learned how to double clutch a five speed when you
could reach the pedals. Seems like a fair trade.
That is your Dad?
I can tell.
You have the same smile.

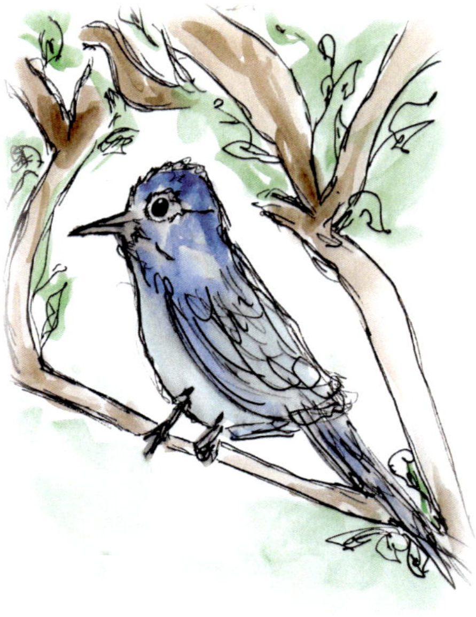

Tree Living

One of the best things about living in this tree?
There is no television. I can tell by the look on your
face that you watched the news and saw another
scared child without her Mom.
You're humans.
You can do better than this.

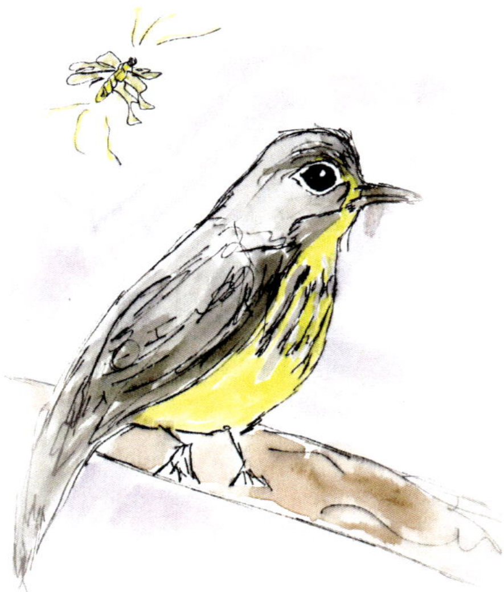

Summer Magic

The most magical part of summer just happened...
I saw my first firefly.

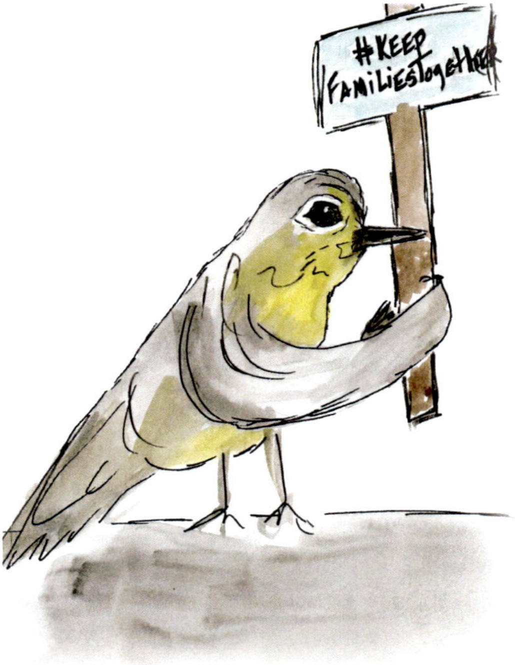
#KEEP
FAMILIESTogether

Standing here in the middle of your driveway, I'm outside of my comfort zone. I feel like I am prey to that nasty crow who always makes me feel like I did him wrong and he is waiting to catch me and scratch my eyes out. But I'm willing to feel uncomfortable so that I can be closer to you and amuse you by twitching my head from side to side. I know how that makes you giggle.

Remember the reoccurring nightmares you used to have when Lily was little? Like the one where you left her on top of the car in her car seat and drove down the highway? Or being separated in a department store with escalators that were made of marshmallows and you would sink into them and never be able to go fast enough to search for her? The horror of it all would jolt you awake only to find her warm little body next to yours. If she was lost, no one would ever know that the only way she falls asleep is if she puts her pointer finger in your mouth. Or that no amount of baby whispering tricks would get her to sleep in her own bed. The not knowing, I imagine that is every parent's nightmare.

So, maybe step out of your comfort zone and scream a little bit about the horrible situation that is happening with migrant children. I know, screaming is not your thing. But do something. You lying there on the lounge chair staring at an empty bird feeder is doing no one any good. Especially me. Those kids must be so scared to not be at home. They must be so scared to not be with someone who loves them before they fall asleep.

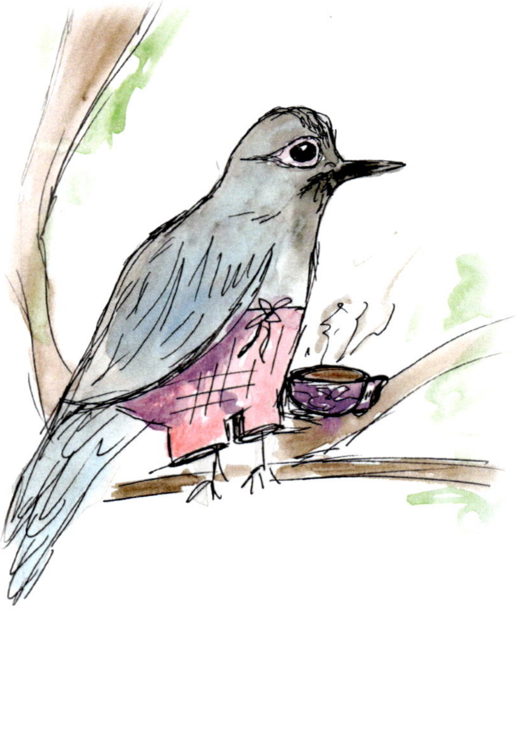

Summer Solstice

Did you hear?
It's the longest day of the year
Fireflies
Blueberry pies
Zucchini blossoms
Backyard possums
The key
for me to stay awake until 9:30?
Sip tea
In this tree
Then it's pink pajamas
For this Mamma

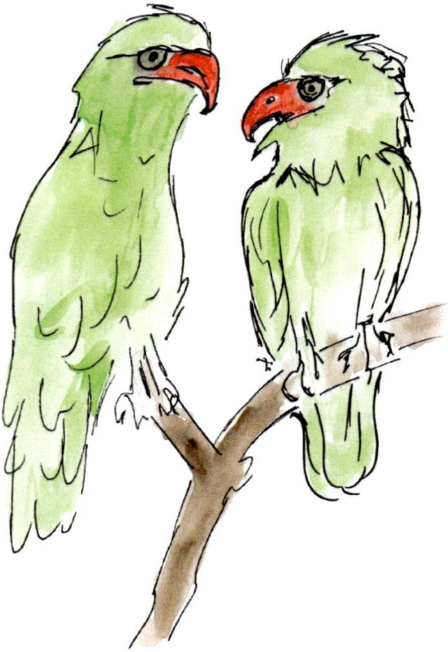

Witches or Sisters

What are those loud, witchy, cackling noises?
Are they coming from inside the house?
Oh geeze.
You AND your sister are in there?
I hope the roof doesn't blow off.
You should have passed out earplugs to your neighbors.
Let the party weekend commence.
Clink. Clink. Cheers to sister love.

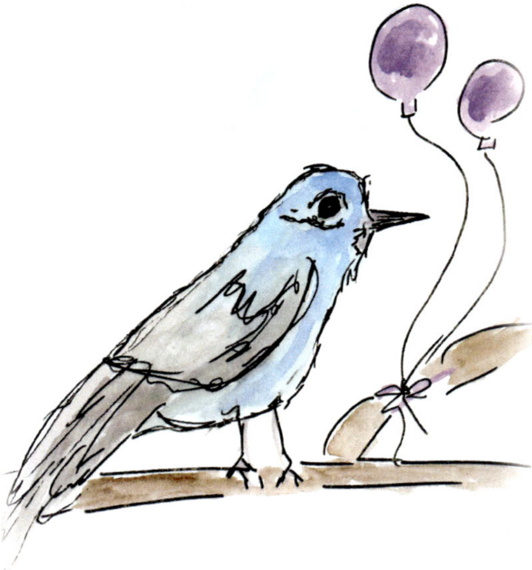

Party Time

Today, finding 10 minutes to crank out a bird
seemed absurd

With all there has been to do
it's finally quiet for a minute or two

Firing up the grill
Beer is on ice to chill

All the preparation is done
You're ready for some fun

Family is here
The Graduate, so beautiful, so dear

Dear God, a tiny request
from me and my guests

Make the rain stop
So this party is not a flop

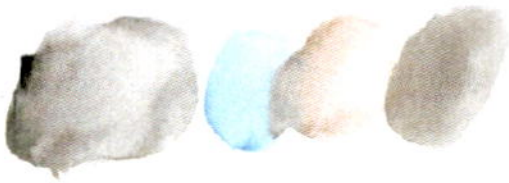

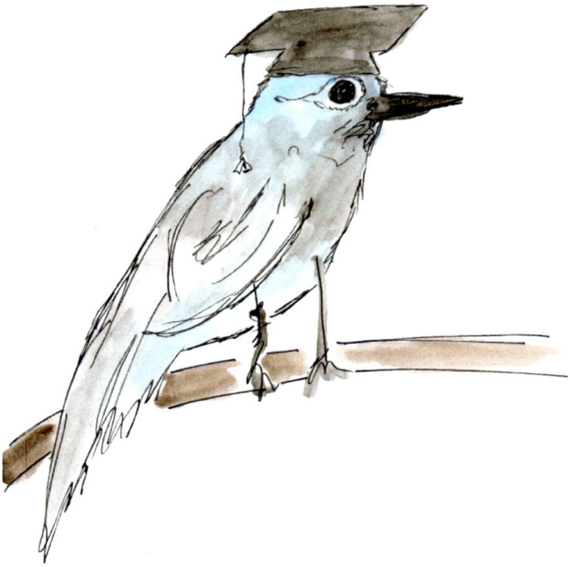

High School Graduate

Thirteen years just went by really really fast.
It's all so cliché.
I blinked and this happened.
Also, I might be a little hungover.
Did someone pour wine in the birdbath yesterday?
Party success.

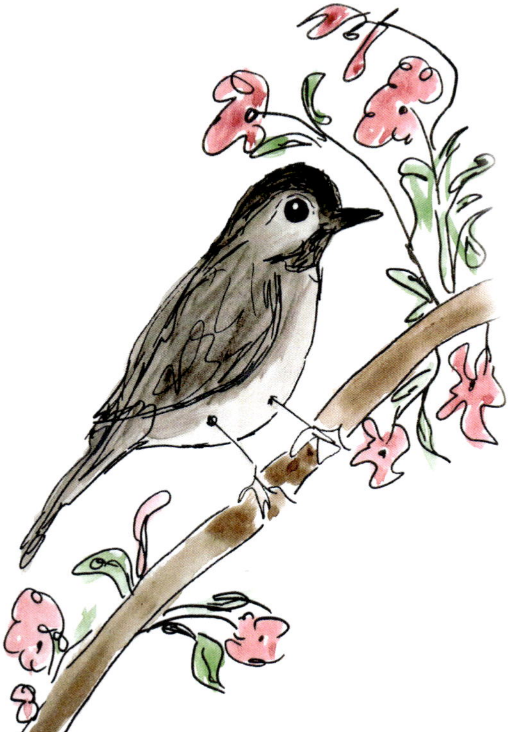

My Family

When they fly away,
I miss them.

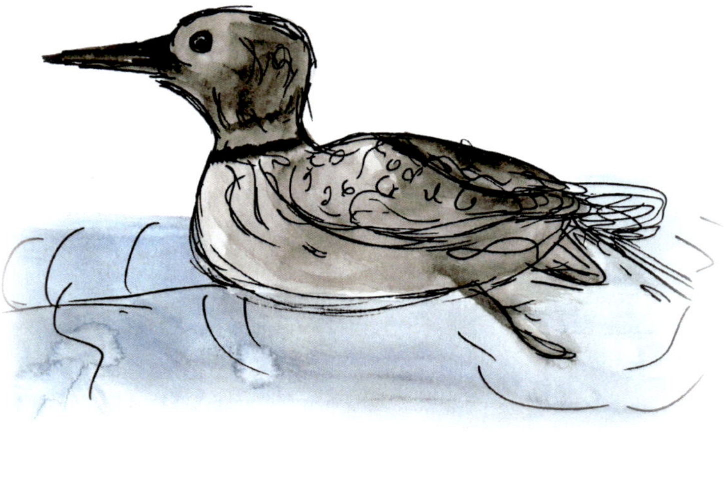

Between Two Loons

Our calls have been called
Mournful
Haunting
Before the day ends
Longing for you
I cry out
Where are you?
You answer
I'm over here
Waiting to kiss you good night

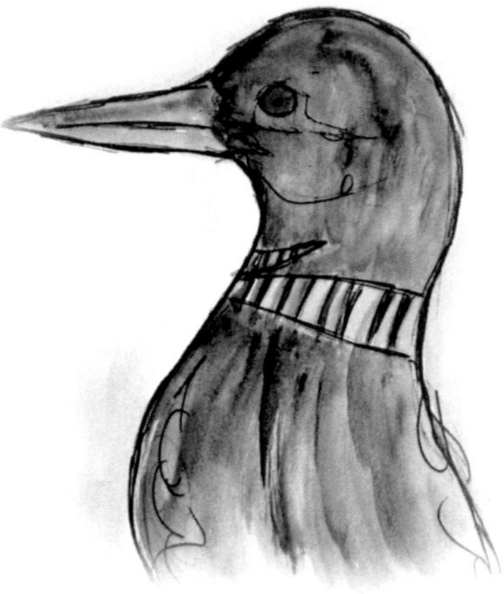

Crazy as a Loon

A Strawberry Moon
in June
doesn't make me sing a different tune
I'm a tiny bit offended by "crazy as a loon"
I haven't been made mad by the power of the moon
I'm not digging through the garbage like a hoodlum raccoon
or staring at you like an ass-scratching baboon
The one I love, my heart, that goon
He sings to me sweetly, my handsome common loon
On the evening before the Strawberry Moon

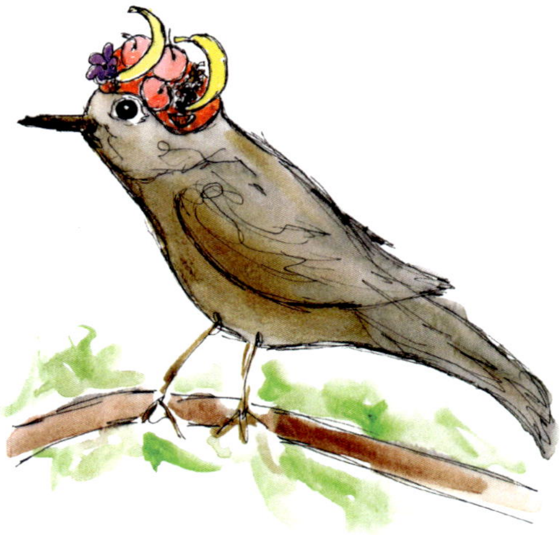

Bananas

You buy bananas every week. They look healthy and adorable hanging from your banana tree fruit rack. You like frozen bananas in your smoothies. Banana bread. Banana and nut muffins. Little cut up banana pieces in your oatmeal. It delights you that it comes in a natural travel case. But to sit there and eat a banana and say, "Wow, I love bananas!" It never happens. It's your fall-back fruit. You're safe with the banana. I do like picking at the pieces that get too squishy and end up in the compost pile but I don't want you to buy any this week. Buy some cherries. Stop playing it safe with the banana. Get wild.

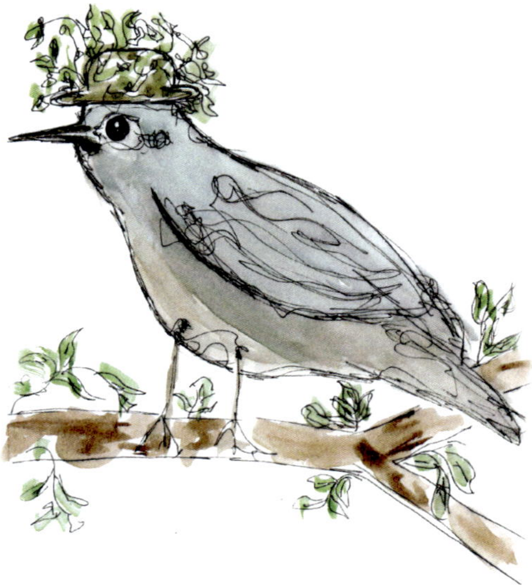

Camouflage

Today I saw two camouflage pickup trucks drive down the road. If they were trying to disguise themselves as a tree, they failed. I saw them. Clear as day. Playing loud rap music also blows the whole blending-into-your-surroundings thing which I thought was the whole purpose of camouflage. They would make terrible spies. I should let them borrow this twiggy leaf hat I made. You can barely see me, right? I'm blending right in.

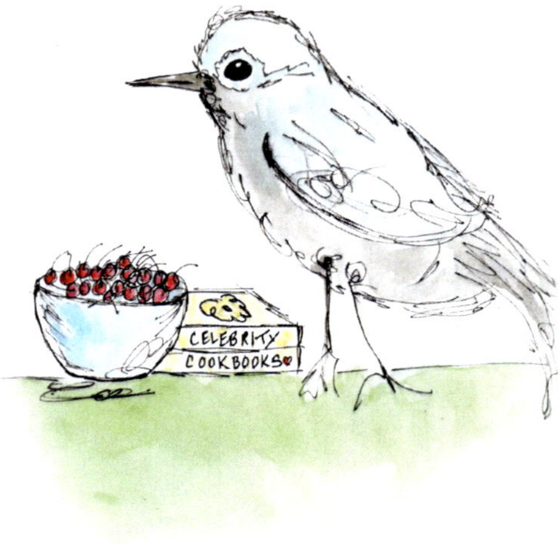
CELEBRITY
COOKBOOKS

Secret Pleasures

Beautiful things happen when it's 95 degrees outside and you choose to have nothing to do but lie on a lounge chair shaded by a big blue umbrella and eat a bowl of cherries while indulging in your secret guilty pleasure. Reading celebrity cookbooks. Don't worry, your secret dorky pleasure is safe with me. And Gwyneth Paltrow and Jessica Seinfeld.

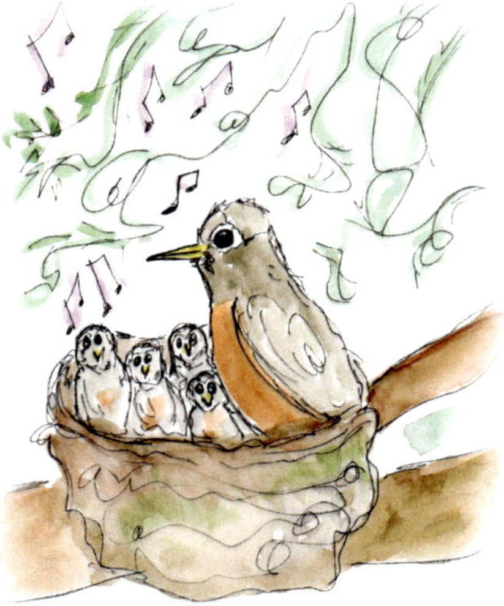

Sleepless Nights

The brightness of the moon and the 1,000 lightning bugs lighting up this pine tree last night like a Pink Floyd laser show woke up the chorus of Cicadas. Who woke up my 4 baby birds. Who wanted a snack. Then another nighttime story. Then they were too hot. Then a fight broke out because someone was touching someone else's wing on purpose even though an invisible line was drawn down the nest which made that space the sacred no-touch zone. The crying. The flashing lights. The all-night cicada singing. Me plus four baby birds in this tiny little nest. For the first time in my life, I was jealous of the Penguin whose only job for a bit is to stand there in the chilly Antarctic breeze, balancing that one baby between their legs while waiting there for their mate to bring food.

This bird stuff is for the birds.

Oh wait.

I'm a bird.

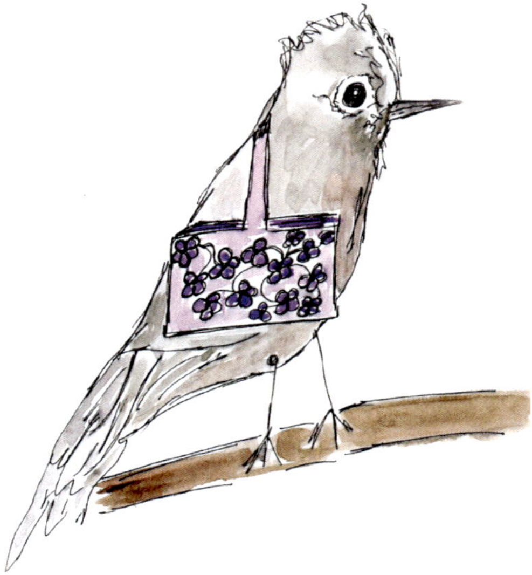

A Mother's Purse

You would not believe the things I can pull out of this purse.
What do you need?
You chilly? I have a balled up cardigan and a scarf.
Headache? Got you covered with 3 medicinal options.
Bleeding? 4 different bandage sizes.
Need some extra light?
I have 10 lightning bugs in a Mason jar.
Hungry? Guess what I have? A banana.
I am Mary Poppins with wings.

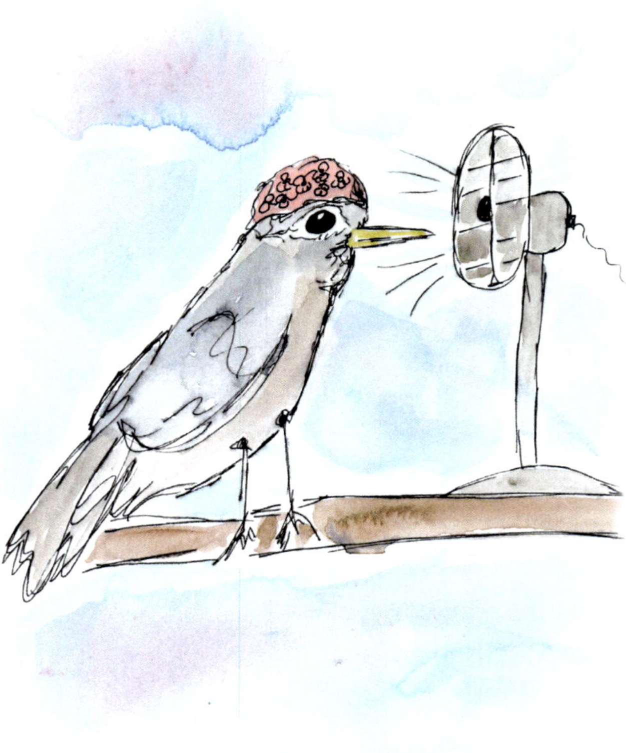

Natural Flow

Once I am up high enough, even on the steamiest days when the air feels thick and unmovable, I can always catch a breeze to glide on. I find that natural flow and then it's cool, smooth sailing. Or I could do what you do and turn the fan on full blast and sit directly in front of it with a cold cloth on my head. One's personal pleasure is such a finicky pursuit.

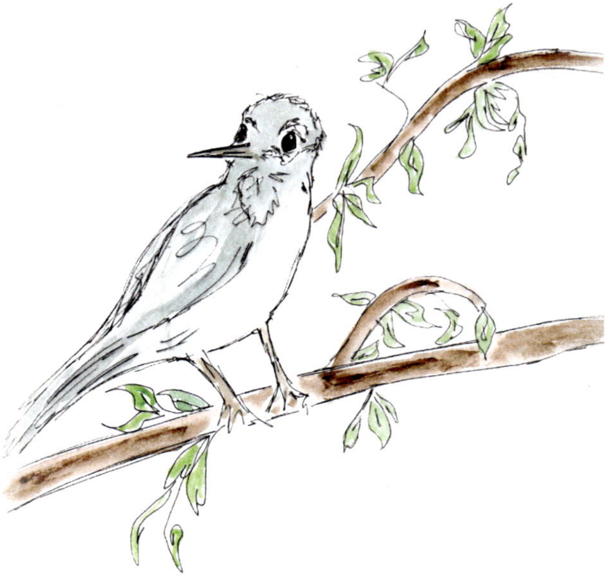

I See London

Perched up here with my bird's-eye view, I've watched you do a lot of things. This morning you realized your skirt was inside-out when you got in the car. You got out and changed things around in the driveway.
This was something new.
I saw your underpants.

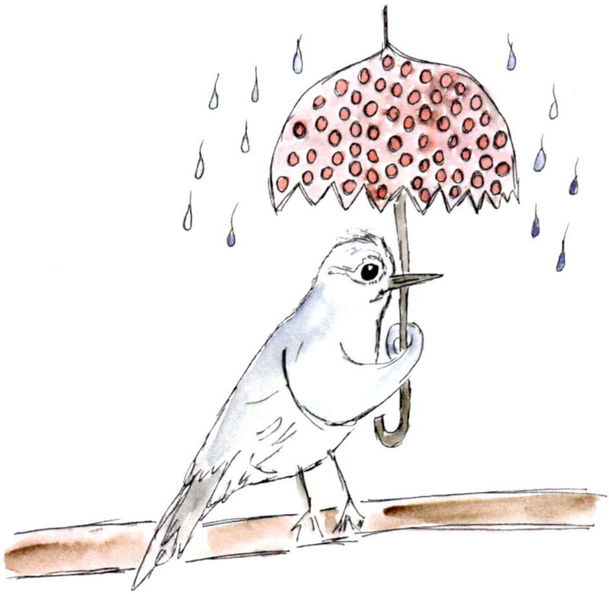

Art's Garage

Flash
One one thousand, two one thousand
Boom
A storm is getting close.

It's one of my first memories from Parrish Lane.
Counting how far out a storm was with Pop-pop.
We sat on nylon lawn chairs near the garage door.

He called me his Little Swede
He called my Dad "Mo"
I don't know why
His name is Dave
"Hey Mo, grab me a beer."

There was a peanut can full of change
on the shelf above the vice grip.
He would let me take a whole handful.
I mostly got pennies.

I dream about the garage a lot.
I can sense that he is there somewhere in the dream
but I've never see him.

Flash
One one thousand, two one thousand
Boom
I always think of him when a storm is coming
Flash
Boom
The storm is here.

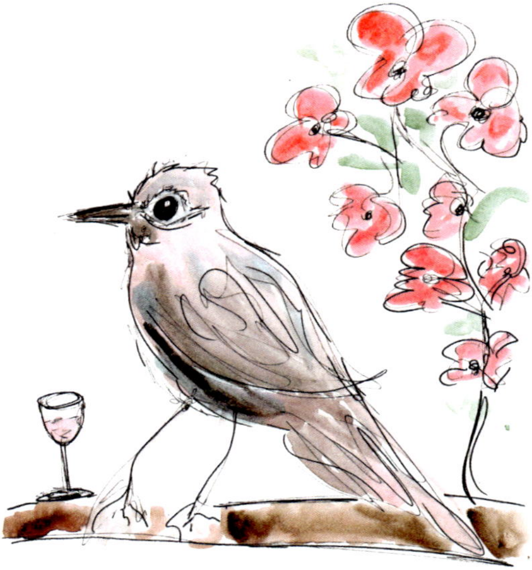

Garden Parties

The best friends are the ones that let you invite yourself over when you're feeling the most vulnerable and hanging on by your fingernails. They don't mind if you stay until the sun sets. These are the til-death-parts-us friends. These are the friends you learn a thing or two from.

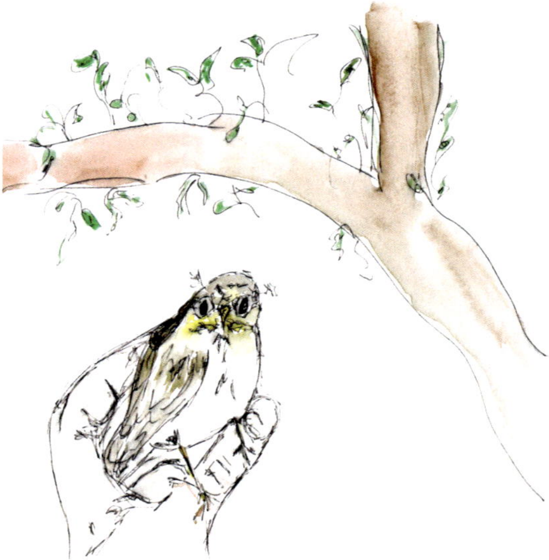

Helping Hand

That wind! Blew us right out of the nest. Toppled the whole thing over! Seems like that was a fail on building a storm-proof nest. My Mom should have borrowed some duct tape. I think my brother landed in the compost pile. Can you give him a hand back up too? I'm close to flying out of here by myself soon. I just need another day to be home and regroup. You're a lifesaver. Literally.

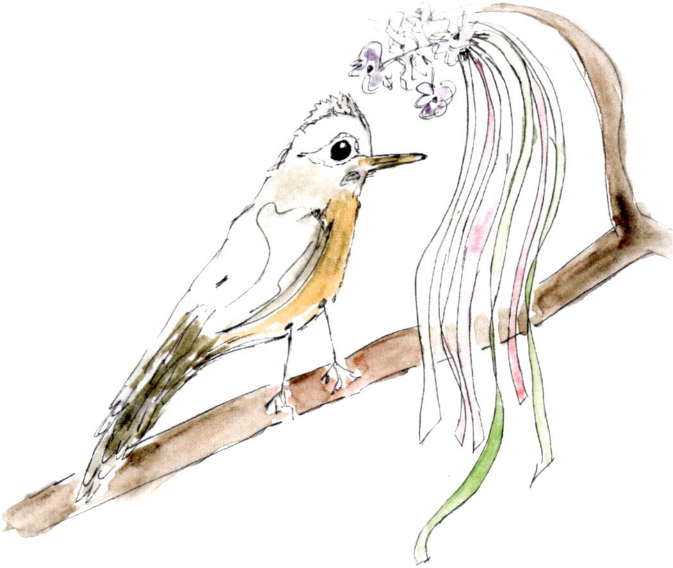

The Right Amount of Sparkle

These are my two post-party favorites: a leftover good morning stale hamburger bun to peck at and the ribbons hanging from the trees. Definitely leave them up. Seeing a flowing little pop of color in the morning from the nest thrills me. And, they're fun to dance with. Having ribbons flowing from your trees is not at all over the top.
It's just the right amount of sparkle.

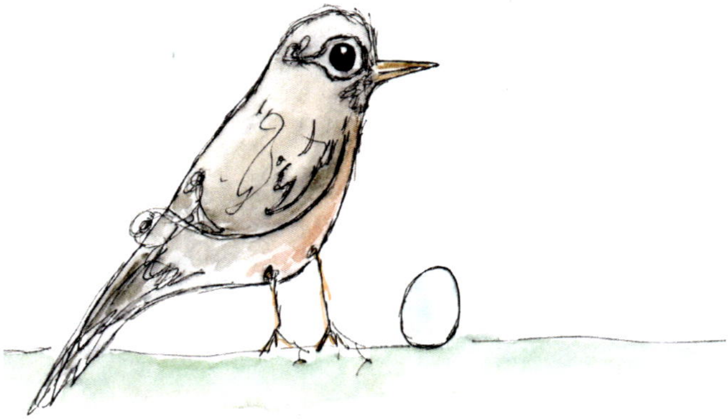

Eggs

There is only a baby bird in an egg that has been fertilized. Sat on. Made warm. Loved a little. Incubated. So, why is it that you hold your breath when you crack an egg in anticipation of a baby chick falling out into your mixing bowl? In all your years of cracking eggs, has this ever happened? No? I didn't think so.

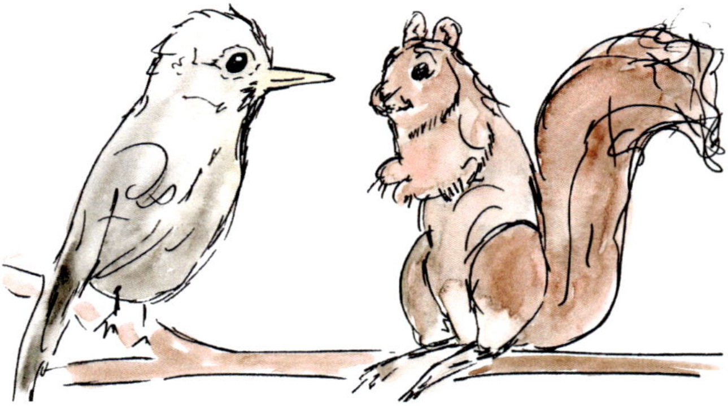

The Chase

The thing I like most about your dog? If given the choice between a bird and a red squirrel, your dog always chooses to chase the red squirrel. Damn fool.
(The squirrel, not the dog)

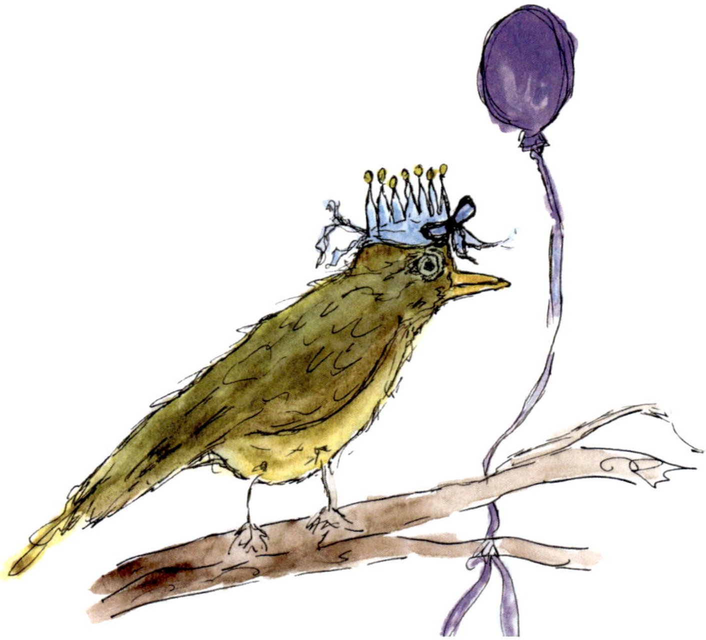

Fifty

Today I am fifty years old. 50!!!!! Half of 100. I'm amused by how it sounds. It doesn't seem to fit me yet. When I started the 100-day project I had no idea that it would be ending on my birthday. I never looked ahead. I just started with Day 1 and showed up. Every day. I never had a stockpile of birds and essays ready to go. Most days I would think of something while I was walking the dog or driving in the car. I noticed that I needed to be outdoors to be inspired. I liked that I called no re-dos or edits. I wouldn't have kept going if I tried to make this anything more than a quick sketch and a couple of words. It was definitely, without a doubt, the most vulnerable thing I have ever done. Who do I think I am to call myself an artist or a writer? Hitting the publish button got easier as I got nice comments from people. I went from having a couple of people reading my blog to 200 a day. I got faster at sketching and started doodling birds with bikinis. I never once felt like the project was a chore.
I love that I did this.

It's ending tomorrow and I am fifty years old.
My daughter is leaving for college next month. These two things are right on the edge of freaking me out but I'm going to continue to show up everyday and figure out what this next part of my life is all about. It's exciting. And scary. But mostly exciting. For both of us. This kid is going to do great things. She's my most beautiful birdy.

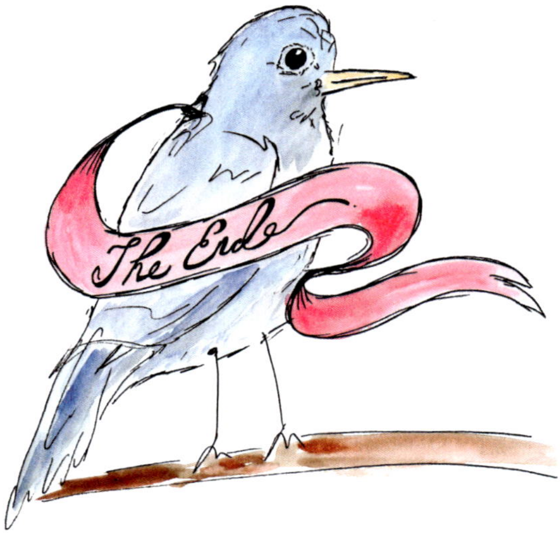
The End

Goodbyes

I'm not good at goodbyes. I might even be the worst goodbyer ever. A goodbye is too much. Too final. I can't bear to think that I'll never see you again. So, I'll give you a high five. Tell you I'll see you in a little bit even though I'm not sure what tomorrow might bring. Then I'll take off and cry like a baby at the thought of not seeing your face again. I'll rush to find a pen to document every detail about our time together so I never forget. Please don't ever forget me either. I already miss you and I'm still right here, watching the whole thing from the top of this tree.